a Bride for Luke

Book #1
Sons of Nora White

CYNDI RAYE

A Bride for Luke

by

Cyndi Raye

Sons Of Nora White

Book #1

A special thank you to one of my readers, Crystal Urchin, for naming the small rural town of River's Edge.

1. http://www.CyndiRaye.com

Table of Contents

Chapter 1

Prologue 1870's

Nora White stood in front of the boarding house on Main Street in Wichita Falls ready to make a deal with the devil. Well, perhaps not the devil. She heard many great things about the matchmaker Miss Addie. She wouldn't be here if she had heard any different. It didn't help her nerves were all over the place.

"Only the best for my sons," she whispered. Her voice caught the wind as a man walked by, tipping the rim of his hat in greeting. "Good day to you, ma'am."

Nora tucked back strands of dark lustrous hair peppered with gray. If there was one thing her husband always said it was she had a great head of hair. A slight smile curved her lips at the nostalgic thought. She still missed Robert so much. He had always taken the time after a long day to place a hand over her cheek and tell her how beautiful she was. He had done it every single day no matter how exhausted he was after a hard day's work on the ranch they owned.

Enough day dreaming, it never got her anywhere. Squaring her shoulders, she stood in front of the big door and lifted a hand to knock.

Before she made contact, the door swung open. A beautiful woman stood there, one of advancing age but well groomed with dark hair and wearing a lovely, expensive gown. "Welcome to Wichita Falls, Mrs. White. Please, do come in."

She held the door open while Nora contemplated spinning around and walking away.

It wouldn't get her sons a good wife if she did so.

Miss Addie led her to the dining room table, offering her a seat while picking up a tray from the side board. "Let's have some tea," she offered, setting a cup in front of Nora.

"Thank you, Miss Addie. I'll get straight to the point. I hear you are the best match-maker in the whole of Texas and beyond. Is this true? I want only the best for my boys."

Miss Addie smiled. "I suppose you are referring to my one hundred percent success rate? You've come to the right place, my dear. Now, what is it you want me to do for you?"

Nora sighed. This Miss Addie was certainly sure of herself. When the decision came upon her to find her sons good Christian women, the others in church told her of Miss Addie's success. She had immediately sent a letter not expecting a reply so fast. Within two weeks, the woman had replied with an appointment to come see her. Two hours later, she found herself smack dab in the middle of the Main Street of Wichita Falls. "I've heard this town is mostly filled with mail-order brides that you are responsible for?"

"You heard correctly. I've chosen the best grooms for the lovely ladies and the most suitable women. This is my life, Miss White. I don't mess around or truffle with tender feelings. You may expect the best, top-notch service from me."

"Thank you."

"Now, tell me about you?"

"Me? Why me? I have no interest in a man? I want this for my three sons."

Miss Addie leaned forward, setting her tea cup on the saucer with a delicate hand. "Miss White, in order for me to find your sons a good, Christian wife, which is what I believe you said, I'll need to know all about the woman who raised them. Fair enough?"

Nora nodded. "I suppose." She didn't like to get personal with others but this was for a good reason. Her sons were her world, her life.

"Tell me about you, Miss White."

"First of all, please, call me Nora. I've been a widow for ten long years now. The boys lost their father and I lost a good, hard-working husband when rustlers tried to steal some of our cattle. He was wounded by one of them and never recovered."

Miss Addie steepled her hands. "I'm sorry for your loss. What is it that brought you to me, Nora?"

"I'm getting older. From the day my husband died, the boys have taken over the ranch. When I tell one of them to go find a nice, sweet Christian woman, they shrug it off, determined to be there for me. I'm not going to be here forever, Miss Addie. I want them each to have a full life with a wonderful woman and not take care of an old lady, but they won't try to find their own happy life."

"You are hardly old, Nora. Why, there are plenty of eligible men who would agree with me."

A blush spread across her cheeks. It had been a long, long time since someone said such a nice thing. "I'm obliged to your kindness, but it's my sons I'm concerned about. Can you help them?"

The noise of a teacup being set on its plate was the only sound in the room right before Miss Addie pushed her chair back. "Of course, I can help. Now, let's take a walk to the porch out front while you tell me who is going to be the first to marry."

Standing on the porch, Nora felt so relieved. Instinct told her she must trust Miss Addie to find the best wife for her oldest son. He was the one she worried about the most. "May as well start with Luke, my oldest. He's been taking care of everyone and everything since Robert's death. Luke is quiet, yet dignified and he is angry."

"Angry? Will this be a potential problem for a bride?"

Nora shook her head. "No, I don't mean he is mean or would hurt anyone. He is so serious all the time. In my heart I'm sure he is angry at his father for leaving us and yet Robert had no control of fate. But he will take care of his bride like he has taken care of the ranch and his brothers. He gives his heart and soul to those he loves. He has a fierce loyalty to all of us."

Miss Addie nodded. "Perhaps he needs a bride who will be willing to show him some kindness. Let me think on this. I'll be in touch."

<><>

A week and a half later a letter arrived. Nora slipped off to her bedroom to read what Miss Addie sent:

Dear Nora,

I do believe I've found the perfect bride for your son, Luke. She has a situation and needs to leave her home town immediately, thus, this letter of urgency sent to you today. It isn't drastic but a choice of hers where she does not wish to marry an ageing friend of the family. I have further investigated and am reassured Miss Abigail Wheatland is all she claims to be.

I've sent her the details and a ticket to arrive in two weeks time. Therefore, you will have the same amount of time to inform your son of his impending marriage. Enclosed, please find a photo of Miss Abigail Wheatland and some other facts about the nuptials. I would have liked to meet your son and spend time with him, which is what I normally do in cases like this. However, since you and I have already met, I've determined you are an honest and upstanding citizen so the need to meet with your son will not take place.

Please inform him of the details of our conversation. Miss Wheatland will arrive expecting to be married immediately. I will expect him to be at the Wichita Falls train station on the sixth of September to fetch her and bring her to the church for the official ceremony.

Yours truly,

Miss Addie

Nora stared at the letter. She thought there would be more time to prepare her son of the upcoming ceremony. Now, she'd have to do it and soon.

Yet, a week and a half later, she was still contemplating what to do. Nora saddled one of the horses. She needed to think. Riding was always her way to explore the vast land her husband had purchased so long ago.

The green hills, valleys and pastures where their cattle grazed made her feel so alive, as if there were no cares in the world. Nora may be ageing but with years in the saddle, she could ride like nobody's business.

Hours later, after refreshing herself with a long jaunt, she slid from the mare, walked her and brushed Fancy Lady down. She smiled at the name for the honey-colored horse. Whenever the mare left the barn, she'd walk as if she was the fanciest girl in town, lifting her tail up in the air along with perking her ears and raising her front feet higher than normal. It always made Nora laugh.

"Glad to see you're smiling," her oldest remarked. He came around the side of the large barn, his tall form intimidating to many except for his mama.

She gave him a look of consternation. "What's that supposed to mean, young man?"

Luke sighed. "Young man? I'm barely young, Mama. Twenty-seven is not young."

Nora grinned. "You are still the most handsome of the boys, you know that, right?"

He rolled his eyes. "Yes, and the most fun, the most original, the best at wrangling cattle and your favorite. You say it to each one of us. At any time any one of us can suddenly become the favorite."

Nora laughed out loud. "You boys are on to me!"

He actually smiled, showing a set of white teeth. "We've known all along."

Nora's way was teasing all three of her boys so they always thought they were the most important. Yet, each one knew how much they were loved in their own right. Her boys were her life but she didn't want them to make her theirs.

They all needed a bride.

It was now or never.

She led Fancy Lady to the coral to graze. After returning to the barn where Luke was brushing down his own horse, she placed a hand over his. "We must talk."

Luke raised an eyebrow, but immediately stopped what he was doing. "What is it? Is something wrong?" Luke stood, throwing the brush on a bale of hay then thrusting his hands deep in the pockets of his pants.

"Maybe we should sit down to talk," Nora warned.

Luke leaned back on his heels. "Let's get this over with right here, Ma. You are looking too serious to waste time finding a seat."

"You are a smart man."

"I'm my mother's son if it is any reassurance." He smiled again, the love for his mother shining in dark eyes.

Nora noticed how handsome he was, how much he looked like her Robert and told him so. "You have your father's smile."

Luke's eyes darkened. He grinded his teeth and frowned. Nora never understood why he seemed to be angry whenever she spoke of Robert. But now was not the time to find out, she had more important things to deal with.

Nora walked to him, taking his hand in her own. She cocked her head and looked at her oldest son, proud of the man he had become. "I know you don't like when I talk of your father and I'm not sure why. Perhaps you are still angry at him for leaving us. It's been ten long years, Luke. It's time to move on. It's time to take the bull by its horns and start new lives."

His eyes widened. "What? Are you trying to tell me you are marrying someone else? I didn't even know you were courting anyone. How did I miss this? Ma, what is this about?"

"There will be a marriage."

"What!"

"But it won't be me."

"What do you mean? What in tar-nation are you trying to tell me then?"

Nora sighed. Her eldest son was so dramatic. He was an angry man, filled with discontentment and yet was the most loyal and trusting one out of all her sons. She imagined Robert would have been so proud of his oldest son. "I've determined none of my boys will ever leave here to try to find a life outside of this ranch. Or," she held up her hand, seeing his mouth start to open wide, "bring a bride here to make a life as I have."

Luke stared. He shook his head. "I don't care about making any other life. I'm perfectly happy right where I am."

"Let me finish. Ranching is a hard, lonely life. When the day is finally over and all the work is done, what do you do?"

He shrugged. "I don't know, either take up with Sam or Adam and play cards with the other hands on the ranch. What does it matter?"

"Luke, you haven't experienced true love. Sitting on the porch, having a glass of lemonade with the person that means the most to you will bring out the best in you. Imagine a walk at night watching the stars, working hard all day to be able to give your wife a kiss when you get home. There's so much more to this life than you are experiencing."

"I don't care about those things."

"You don't because you haven't experienced them. Luke, I've taken matters in to my own hands."

He turned. "Ma, what did you do?"

She nodded, determined to make him understand. "I've sent for a mail-order bride for you, Luke. Please, before you refuse, just please give it a chance."

"No."

"It's too late, she is already on her way here."

He shoved his fists deeper in his pockets. She almost smiled at the way some things never changed. He'd been doing that since he was five years old and found out he had pockets in the britches he wore.

"What? You can't order a mail-order bride and not even ask me! Besides, what kind of woman would do such a thing as come out to the West not knowing what she was getting?"

He pulled his hands out and then they went back in his pockets. Soon, he'd balance himself on his heels.

"A woman who is forced to marry an old man three times her age by parents who only want the money the marriage promises, that's who. There are even worse stories I'm told."

She actually noticed a worried look cross his face. Her son actually had some emotion when it came to other people besides his own family. What a nice surprise to realize. She'd have to play on that, even though it wasn't nice to do so. But he wasn't giving her much choice. His refusal was expected but this was harder than she had thought.

Was she doing the exact same thing his bride's family was doing? Forcing a marriage on two people who didn't want to be married? Biting the side of her bottom lip, Nora was determined to see her sons happy and they would never do this on their own. She had to help them. It was a whole different situation than the brides.

"The contract from the match-making agency is clear. You must marry immediately upon meeting, however, if, after three months, you both wish to part ways, there will be an annulment granted as long as the marriage bed is still pure."

"No."

"Didn't you hear what I said?"

"The answer is still no."

She wasn't going to drag him to the alter. He had to at least want a small part of this. What was she able to dangle in front of him to convince him to give it a try?

"I'll give your father's pistol to you if you agree to try this for three months."

"Agree."

"I know it's not exactly what you, what did you say?"

"Agree. I've wanted that pistol every since Samuel said he was going to claim it last year."

Nora blinked. "You would marry this bride so you can get one up on your brother?"

Luke nodded. "Kind of looks that way, huh?"

Nora threw her hands up in the air. "Oh, for Pete's sake! If that's all I had to do, well, then when it comes time to have the talk with your brothers, tell me what they want?"

Luke backed up, his hands out in front of him. "Now, Ma, do not make me tell my brother's secrets."

Nora smiled. She knew Luke would tell her. If he had to get married, he'd make darn sure it was going to happen to his brothers as well. "It's a yes, then?"

"Of course."

She placed her hands on her hips, a smile from ear to ear. "Well then, be ready to pick up your new bride at eight-thirty Saturday morning at the train station in Wichita Falls."

"So soon?"

"I'm afraid so. Now, what is it the other boys want most of all?"

Luke shook his head. "I'll tell you when the time is right." He straightened up, a serious look on his face. "Ma, even though I'm getting married, you will always be my favorite girl."

A tear slipped down Nora's cheek. Her first born would always be special, too. Instead of telling him that, she wrapped her arms around his neck and gave him a big old hug. "I love you, son. You know I'm doing this for you. All I want is for you to be happy."

"I know, Ma."

Chapter 2

Luke held the reins in his left hand as he pulled the buggy to a stop near the Wichita Falls rail road station. At twenty-seven all he ever knew was the family ranch. Ever since his Pa died ten years ago, Luke found himself in charge. He was determined his Ma would never find out their father's secret and so far the three brothers had been able to hide it well. It was one of the reasons bringing a wife into the mix will cause complications, let alone three wives in all. He wasn't about to let it happen.

Luke left the buggy sitting along the street and walked to the train depot. It gave him time to think. The September breeze rustled the small bushes and trees along the path. Main Street in Wichita Falls was pretty quiet for this time of day.

Maybe because it was Saturday. Most families were at home enjoying their breakfast while he already had his and was about to get married. Eight-thirty in the morning was too darn early to get hitched.

Luke leaned his tall frame against the railing while he waited for the whistle that alerted the town of the incoming train. He fingered his Pa's gun with the pearl handle hanging in the holster on his right hip underneath his good Sunday jacket. A smile played across his mouth as he pictured the look on Samuel's face the moment he noticed the gun.

Luke didn't really care too much about keeping it. He figured he'd tease his brother, get him back for some of the tricks Samuel did to him. Eventually, he'd give the gun to Samuel. He'd also appease his Ma with three months of a marriage he had no intention of following through with. After that, he hoped his Ma would finally realize all Luke wanted was to take care of the ranch. He didn't need a woman to interfere in their lives.

Luke's little brother Samuel was an expert at shooting guns. He provided plenty of game and meat for the ranch on a daily basis. His Pa had always praised Samuel's shooting skills whenever they were together. It was probably the one thing his brother had cherished about the times with their Pa.

Luke sighed as the rails began to rattle. The locomotive was almost here. She was almost here. On that train was the woman he was about to marry for three months. What kind of lady puts herself out there not knowing anything about a man except for the fact he owns a ranch with his brothers and Ma?

As the oldest, his duty was to protect the ranch and his family. He also had to appease his mother or she'd never give up trying to find a wife for all of them. He hoped this three month trial would make her realize marriage wasn't in the cards for any of them. Luke was going to make sure of it.

Lucky for Luke he didn't have to worry about being nice. Most people considered him a grump anyway. He heard the talk and didn't care. For as long as he remembered if he kept to himself and didn't talk much, the secrets of his family were safe. Anyone getting too close would be pushed out.

This notion of marrying a mail order bride was one of his Ma's grand ideas. She kept saying how old she was getting and wanted to see them all happy. As far as Luke was concerned he'd be happier if no one minded his business.

The scowl on his face was probably the first thing his new bride-to-be would see, but he didn't try to make it disappear. She may as well get used to it.

When he felt a presence, Luke looked up in surprise. His boots were stuck on the platform. The woman who stood in front of him was more beautiful than anyone he'd ever seen before. Her hair was so black it looked like there were shades of blue highlighting it. Her skin was like porcelain. He almost reached out to touch her ruby colored lips. He stared into her doe shaped eyes, mesmerized by their beauty.

"Hello," she said, her voice as pretty as a songbirds.

Luke stared.

She tilted her head and stared back, then cracked a huge smile. "You must be Mr. Luke White. Hello, I'm Abigail Wheatland. How do you do?"

She held out her hand. He took it, dropping a soft kiss on her gloved hand. She took a step back.

"Hello," he finally mastered his voice. "I'm Luke."

"It's a pleasure to finally meet you," she said, as if they had been plotting and planning this meeting for months and yet it had only been two weeks.

He didn't dare fall into her trap. She was a witch, had to be. Her dark eyes bore into his putting some kind of darn spell on him. He shook himself, puffed out his chest and pushed his hat back. Spell or not, he couldn't afford to let this happen.

"Let's get to the church, time's a wasting," he told her, unsmiling. Holding out his arm, she gave him a look of confusion then snapped her lovely mouth shut and tucked her arm in his.

"I trust you have read the rules?" Her voice was kind yet business like.

"I did. Here are my rules, Miss Wheatland. I have no intention of taking you to the marriage bed. My Ma wants me married. I don't want to be but because she is the most wonderful woman on the planet, I am appeasing her at the moment. In three months, we will have our marriage annulled."

She stopped dead. "I'm certain those words you are spewing are not meant for me."

"What? Of course they are."

"I am sorry. If you want to fool your Ma it is your business. I am not going to marry a man who has no intention of keeping his end of the bargain."

"Miss Wheatland. You are wrong. You wanted out of marrying an old man. I want to appease my mother. We both have our needs and can help each other. I'm sure you can speak to Miss Addie in a month or two and tell her our marriage isn't working and to find you someone else by the time of our annulment."

"I see you have it all figured out. I suppose I have no say in the matter?"

They were almost at the church. Luke turned to her. "Look, I don't like people. I'm not nice. I like being out on the range away from everyone. I'd make a terrible husband. My life is on the ranch, by myself. Nothing more will ever take its place. I'm trying to be upfront with you before we walk through those doors."

Luke figured it would scare her off. Perhaps even get her back on the train so he could go back and tell his Ma she had changed her mind. He'd give his brother the pearl-handled pistol and get back to ranching.

Instead, she squeezed his arm. "Let's get on with it, then." Her kind, beautiful eyes sparkled.

Luke was mesmerized. He stood there, staring into her eyes like a dumbstruck child.

She coughed. Placing a gloved hand over her mouth, Miss Wheatland coughed again, shaking him from the spell she most likely put on him.

She wasn't backing down. He didn't scare her off. Even though it was better if she ran the other way, he had to admit she had gumption marrying someone like him.

Abigail was afraid her teeth would rattle so loud the small gathering of strangers at the front of the church would hear. She was biting down on them, trying to keep herself from giving her groom a what for! How dare he assume she wanted to annul the marriage!

Instead of giving him a saucy piece of her mind, she gazed at him with one of the sweetest smiles she was able to muster. He would have to learn she was no one to trifle with.

Everyone knew Abigail was kind, generous and loving to most everyone she knew. When she got her dander up though, it was another story and by darned if this man got her riled from the get go.

Abigail was annoyed more than anything. Yes, he did manage to save her from a fate worse than death but that didn't mean he could marry her then throw her out like yesterday's biscuits.

What if she wanted to stay married to him? What if they fell in love?

"You may kiss the bride." Abigail had missed most of the ceremony, automatically agreeing and repeating the reverend's words. Instead, her head had been filled up with so much she hadn't been paying attention.

When she turned to her new husband, he was staring at her as if seeing her for the first time. It was obvious he stood there waiting to kiss her. The words they had spoken a few moments ago were forgotten when he dipped his head and brushed his mouth over hers.

Abigail wanted to show him a thing or two. To be honest with herself, she wanted to know if he was attracted to her at all. He came off as if he wasn't but she had to know.

She pushed her mouth harder on to his, taking a step closer. All of a sudden, his two arms were wrapped around her shoulders, his lips pressed harder against hers. Abigail was pleasantly surprised at his reaction. Perhaps he did think she was kissable after all. Even if he had no plans to make the marriage last more than three months, at least his kisses were pleasant.

Her hands instantly went to cup his face. She liked his kisses, a lot. But before she got to like them too much, he pulled back as if a whip had cracked him on the side of the head.

Five other complete strangers looked on, amused. The only thing Abigail was able to do was give them all a pleasant smile. After all, she was a married woman now, there was no reason to feel ashamed of a kiss like this one.

Luke bent close to her ear. "Your kisses are wonderful but it won't change my mind."

When she looked up at him, she saw amusement on his face. She smiled. "We best be on our way to the ranch, don't you think so, Mr. White?"

The others congratulated the new couple, promising to come visit soon. They all had prior arrangements for the day but were happy to take the time to witness a marriage. Abigail figured she'd never see them again after this. She had no idea how people behaved in a small town.

One of the ladies introduced herself as Miss Addie, her match maker. "Welcome to Wichita Falls, dear. Now, I know you are not used to small towns, being you are from the big city of Philadelphia but we all look out for each other here. If you have any issues at all, please, come see me. I own the boarding house a few doors down."

When Miss Addie said if there were any issues to come see her, she didn't miss the fact the older woman looked directly at her new husband. Her brow went in the air. "Is there something I need to be aware of?" Abigail asked.

"No, I don't think you have anything at all to worry about. Especially not after the kiss we all witnessed. But I like to make sure all of my brides know I am here if need be."

"Thank you. I will come visit, perhaps in a month or two to let you know how we are faring." When Abigail said this, she looked right into Luke's eyes, who shifted away. He seemed uncomfortable all of a sudden.

Miss Addie didn't miss a trick either. The thoughtful look on her face made Abigail realize the woman paid much more attention than what anyone realized. This was good, at least she hadn't paired Abigail with a man who was worse than the one she had left in Philadelphia.

As they exited the church, Abigail stumbled on the wooden walk. She held a hand to her head as a wave of dizziness swept over her. Luke reached out to take her elbow. "Are you alright?"

"I'm sorry. I believe in my rush to get here I hadn't eaten since yesterday."

Luke nodded. "Well then, let's be off to Jenna's Cafe to fix the problem before heading back."

Abigail frowned. "You believe I am a problem?"

Luke shook his head and smiled. "Not one bit, Mrs. White." He leaned in and whispered in her ear, "but only for three months."

"Not funny," she shot back.

He gave her a genuine smile and held out his arm. She once again tucked her hand into his as they made their way to the small café sitting alongside a large three story hotel.

Jenna greeted them with her usual happy go lucky attitude. "Good morning folks. Come right in and have a seat. It's not too busy today since it's Saturday."

They settled in the first table near a large picture window. Abigail was curious. She had never been to a pioneer town before. Her gaze fell upon the saloon across the street and watched as the barkeep swept the front porch, a towel thrown haphazardly across one shoulder.

"I hear congratulations are in order for our newly married couple. So, breakfast is on me."

Abigail was taken back. "How did you know? We literally just got married?"

Jenna leaned down with a smile. "I hear you are from Philadelphia? Well, this town is like nothing you've ever seen before. Everyone knows current business as soon as it happens. Trust me, I was shocked as well when I first came here. You will be fine."

Abigail was not used to people knowing her business. In Philadelphia, life there was fast-paced. People hurried everywhere, ignoring other folks in their path. It was not often anyone tipped a hat these days except maybe in circles she wasn't accustomed to.

She hoped the ranch Luke was taking her to was a good distance from this town. Even though she genuinely liked people, it was strange to her that people knew all about her. Did she want others knowing so much about her life? Abigail certainly was not used to country living.

There were a lot of things she hadn't previously thought of before taking this journey and accepting the mail order bride proposal. When she agreed to the three-month arrangement, Abigail hadn't given it much thought. In her mad dash to be away from old Mister Banners, any deal had been welcomed.

"Here you are, fresh eggs easy over and sour dough bread for dipping. Welcome to Wichita Falls, Mrs. White." Jenna gave her a huge smile and left them to eat.

The food was really good. Abigail was hungry. She put her head down and ignored Luke as she filled her belly with the warm food. Finally, she scraped the last of her eggs from the plate, dabbed a napkin over her mouth and set it down on the table as she released a sigh. "Delicious!"

Luke grinned. "It's good to see you are a hearty eater," he told her. "My boys at the ranch can't put down a meal that quick!"

"Are you saying -"

He held up his hand. "I'm not saying anything except I'm glad you like to eat."

Jenna stopped to refill the cups. She leaned down and looked at Luke, shaking her head back and forth. "Luke, I've known you since I've opened my café and you never tell a woman she is a hearty eater. That's like telling her she eats too much."

Her words were meant for him but she said it loud enough Abigail heard. "It's alright, Jenna. I'm starting to get use to Mr. White's way of talking."

Jenna looked at her. "It's never alright when someone speaks like a fool. Mr. White owes you an apology."

The two sitting across from each other were left staring after Jenna as she went to the next table. It was Abigail who broke a smile first. "Is she for real? How did she even hear what you said to me?"

"Seems everyone in this town knows everything. We better head back to the ranch."

As they walked out the door, Luke turned back, stating loud enough for Jenna and the other guests to hear. "I'm sorry if I offended your sensibilities, Mrs. White."

Abigail responded. "Luckily for you, I am not eating so heartily right now there's room to accept your apology."

She caught Luke's face from the corner of her eyes. He shook his head, took her elbow and helped her into the buggy. It was time to find out what was in store for her next. She hoped the rest of his family was more pleasant than him.

Chapter 3

Two hours later, Luke turned the buggy off the main road on a wide lane that led to the White Ranch. Out front on a small metal gate swung partially opened, the name of their property was imprinted over top in thick, bold letters.

They traveled for awhile until he pointed. "That's the main house, Ma's house, where she lives along with my two brothers."

She turned to stare at the large two-story house. It was plenty big for a large family. As they got closer, bluebonnets were scattered haphazardly in the yard surrounding the wrap around porch. Daisy's took up the flower bed, along with small blotches of lavender. "It's lovely."

He turned the buggy to the left where a faded gravel road crossed over the yard towards the barn and a coral, along with a few other buildings that Abigail had no idea what they were.

The buggy kept on for awhile until Luke stopped in front of a log cabin structure. More bluebonnets grew in patches all around the cabin. It was less than half the size of the family house. She hadn't seen it sitting amongst the row of trees at first. He held out a hand for her. "We're home."

"What? Home? Here?" What about the big family home where there would be people? This cabin was set back against the property surrounded on three sides by what looked like some brush and trees and near a small brook. If Abigail hadn't been nervous before she was now at the thought of them being isolated from the rest of the family.

He shrugged, waiting for her to take his hand. "I'm afraid so, this here is my place."

"Your place? Why, I was under the impression we would live with your Ma until the three months were up." Abigail turned back, seeing the white clap board main house in the far distance. She would be able to walk if she had to but it looked so far away at the moment.

"I built this log cabin a few years ago. It sits along the edge of our property line." He pointed to the long expanse of meadow past the cabin, separated by a four foot fence made of wooden posts and wire. "That's the neighbors land. We stay away from beyond the row of trees there."

Abigail walked alongside him as he showed her around the place. There was a small well house along side the cabin where some of the food was stored as well as a lean to for firewood and shelter for the horse and buggy. She took everything in before heading back to the buggy.

"Where are you going?"

"To get my things. I hope this cabin has more than one bedroom." She reached in the back to pull out her carpetbag. A hand clasped over hers.

"Let me," he offered. Luke picked up her bag as if it weighed nothing. She knew better. Most of her belongings were in there, along with some presents she brought from Philadelphia. She hadn't had time to bring anything more.

"Thank you." Luke headed for the door, turning the round iron knob. It opened easily enough. She thought it was odd not to lock the door but supposed out here in the country there wasn't many people to break in. Not like the city where robberies happened all the time and some homeless urchins crawled through open windows to forage food.

Inside, a large open room caught Abigail's eyes. A large fireplace took up an area on one side of the wall, and a small settee with another arm chair were placed around a rug in front of the fireplace. It was a bit rough yet cozy and looked as if a woman had put some finishing touches here and there.

"My Ma decorated for me," he told her, unashamed to admit such a thing.

"She did a nice job."

"You will love her, I'm sure."

"I hope so," Abigail mumbled. She waltzed around the kitchen area, glad to see tidy rows of supplies on shelves near the cook stove. A large table was centered in the middle of the kitchen area with several chairs pushed tight against. Another large rug covered the floor underneath the table and plaid curtains hung over the small window.

"Come along, Abigail. I'll show you the rest of the house."

She followed her new husband through another solid wood door. It opened into a large bedroom where a four poster wooden framed bed sat. A beautiful quilt covered the bed, with matching curtains. A large dresser with several drawers stood underneath the single bedroom window. Another fireplace was built into the far wall. "There's one in here, too?"

"Yes, it helps to keep the chill out on some cool evenings. You won't need it much but will be glad it's there on occasion."

Abigail noticed a rocking chair sitting haphazardly in front of the fireplace. A small desk and stool was tucked into another corner. An old antique trunk sat on the floor, butted up against the foot of the bed. Abigail ran a hand over the top. "This is a beautiful trunk."

"You can put your things in it if you'd like. Ma insisted I keep it." Abigail noticed some bitterness in his voice but forgot the tone when she opened it up to find cedar lined the walls inside. It was the perfect size to place her clothing.

She accepted the carpet bag and turned to him. "Thank you."

When he stood there, not leaving, she tilted her head. He still didn't move. She coughed, placing a hand over her mouth.

He had been staring at the trunk for such a long time she began to worry. "Luke, is there something wrong?"

He still stared at the trunk, as if in a trance. She stood beside him, placing a hand on his arm. The touch of her hand caught him unaware. Luke turned to her with tortured eyes. When he realized how much his emotions were showing, his face quickly changed to a blank expression.

Should this worry her? She let go of his arm, taking a step back. Luke seemed to need a moment to recover so she turned away, placing her carpet bag on the bed and opened it up. Pulling a gown out, she shook it, her back to him, then laid it on the bed. She was so glad the trunk was so large so she wouldn't have to fold the gown so small like she had done on the way here.

"I'll leave you to your work," he told her and quickly left the room. Abigail turned to the now closed door, wondering what all that was about. He seemed genuinely upset when she had opened the trunk. What was it about this certain piece of furniture that distressed a man so?

Abigail finished placing her belongings in the truck, then closed its huge lid and left her gifts on the bed cover. She wandered out to the living room to find Luke standing by the window in the kitchen, staring out. His fists were thrust in his pockets, his arms stiff.

"Luke, is there something bothering you?" she asked, her gentle voice causing him to turn his head. He let out his breath, his shoulders dropping as if he had a heavy burden placed there.

"That trunk belonged to my parents. My father carved it for Ma. I remember the day he gave it to her and how happy it made her. I guess I was reminiscing about the days when he was alive. I think I've been so angry at him for leaving us, I forgot about all the wonderful moments, too. I'm sorry, I did not mean to upset you."

She stood behind him, placing a gentle hand on his shoulder. "Sometimes it's good to think of those wonderful memories, Luke."

"It's been ten years. You'd think I'd be over him by now."

She smiled then leaned her head on his shoulder. "Sometimes it takes a lifetime. Holding anger inside makes the pain linger on and on. Would you like to talk about why you are angry?" She knew it was a touchy subject and yet the bond they were forming in this moment felt right.

He ran a hand through thick, dark hair. "I can't. There's no sense in thinking about the past. Ma has dinner waiting. She wants to meet you so we best get moving."

Abigail knew he was done talking. She wasn't about to give up on him though. He was holding something inside of him that was tearing up his heart, breaking it in two. His voice, his eyes, they held his secret demons, the pain was clear to see. "I'm looking forward to meeting her as well. I have a gift for everyone, I'll be right back."

When Abigail turned to go to the bedroom for her gifts, she hadn't realized his arm had been around her shoulder. He held her there for a second. "Thank you, Abigail. I'm not sure what just happened, but your words softened my soul somewhat."

She smiled at her husband. He was going to throw her out in three months time whether she wanted to go or not. Maybe they would bond more and he'd change his mind. She rather liked being here right now. But if he didn't change his mind, she'd have to guard her heart. It was so confusing but anything was better than living with a man three times her age.

The buggy ride to the main house was interesting. Two men, high-tailing it across the prairie raced towards the white two story. Hooping and hollering went on until Luke's buggy pulled up. The men raced towards them. Abigail's heart began to pound. Who were these men? His brothers? If so, they seemed a bit on the wild side.

An older woman came outside, standing on the porch with hands on her hips. They all watched as the two men jumped from the horses and raced across the yard, heading towards the water pump.

Abigail gasped. "Oh, dear. The one in the blue shirt just tripped the other man. He is, oh, my!"

"You cheater!"

"You cheated first!"

Luke grinned.

The two went tumbling across the yard like one of the many tumble weeds that danced across the prairie.

His mother stood on the porch. "Luke, best break up the two before they're sporting black eyes." She barely looked at Abigail, but then said, "Welcome to the White Ranch, dear. We'll be introduced in a few minutes."

Luke shook his head, letting Abigail stand there staring. He walked towards the two men.

In a matter of seconds, Luke jumped into the fray. Abigail covered her mouth with her hand. Three men now tumbled around the yard. No one threw a fist but wrestled as if they were fighting a bear.

"You'd think after working the ranch hard all day they'd be too tired to act like a bunch of youngsters. May as well get used to this, these boys of mine will never grow up."

Abigail stood on the porch beside Luke's mother. "How often does this happen?"

Nora White grinned. "At least once a week. Seems Samuel and Adam get to racing home and then one of them cheats. Now its a free for all. I better get in and check the pot of stew. Come on in, I'll show you around."

Abigail took one look back and decided to follow the older woman. The three men were on the ground, huffing and puffing and laughing like a bunch of school boys. "It doesn't look like anyone won that round."

Nora nodded. "No one ever wins. Besides, I've learned over the years they do this so they can speak in secret to each other. While we are inside, they are hunched together talking about things they want no one to know about. Hello, dear. I'm Luke's mother, Nora. Please don't call me Mrs. White. I am Nora to you now that you are my daughter."

Nora took both of Abigail's hands in her own. They were warm hands that gave comfort. She turned back to her boys before stepping through the door. "I expect to see three men cleaned up and ready to eat in five minutes."

Abigail smiled. Nora hadn't raised her voice. When she spoke, her sons stopped what they were doing. As Abigail went inside, she noticed they began brushing off their pants, working their way towards the water pump one at a time.

"Come along, Abigail." Nora led her to the kitchen where a big pot of stew was simmering. The house was set up similar to the cabin except on a much larger scale. With a longer table, a few benches and chairs around the wooden oblong table, Abigail was certain this table was where everyone shared supper each night.

"You have a lovely home, Nora."

Nora handed her a towel. "Thank you. I made some cornbread. Would you mind taking it out of the oven?"

"Yes, of course." Abigail set to work, helping her mother-in-law finish dinner. She waited while Abigail leaned out the door and rang the dinner bell. The sound of the bell chiming was so loud she covered her ears.

Nora looked back and smiled. "Get used to the noise, Abigail. It will get much louder in a few minutes."

One by one Luke and his brothers came inside, standing beside a chair at the table. Abigail was introduced to Samuel and Adam, who each shook her hand.

Samuel was the first to speak up. "We were just told our brother got married this morning. Welcome to the family."

Adam nodded and sat down right before three other men made their way to the table next. Then, out of the blue, an older man entered, placing his hat on the hook beside the door. "Miss Nora, Ma'am," he said, nodding first to Luke's Ma and then her. Each man introduced himself before taking their place at the table.

"Mrs. White, I'm Cody, one of the ranch hands. Nice to meet you." Cody was young, probably in his early twenties if that. He had sandy hair and a serious face. Abigail nodded.

"I'm Roger, ma'am, a pleasure," he said, showing off a set of dark brown curls when he took off his hat.

Luke spoke up. "Roger is an expert with horses. You'll find him mostly in the stables."

"My pleasure," Abigail said. This whole group was like one happy family. They all appeared comfortable in Nora's kitchen.

"I'm Matt, another one of the ranch hands, Mrs. White. Pleased to meet you." He stood beside Roger, eyes on the food. Abigail almost laughed. He looked so hungry, like he wanted to grab his food and run.

An older man came to the table, sporting a limp. He nodded curtly, the red hair on his head pasted against his skull. He held out a weathered hand. "Nice to meet you, Mrs. White. I hope you can make that one smile once in awhile. He's been grumpy for the last ten years."

"My pleasure, sir. I'll do my best," Abigail told him. He was a crusty old man, with a devil may care attitude. She knew instantly she'd like him.

Nora cleared her throat. "Now, Rusty, be kind. Let's pray." Everyone took hands while Nora led them in a short but sweet prayer. The moment the last word left her mouth, the sound of chairs and benches scraping against the floor echoed through the kitchen. Hands reached for the corn bread while bowls were passed around the table.

Abigail watched in wonder as the men gobbled down the food. It probably took all of five minutes for them to finish their plates. When she looked up Nora White's eyes were on her. "Welcome to the family, Abigail."

"Here, here!" Each man held up their drinking cup. Her husband lifted his, staring at her, his dark eyes unreadable. She was honored they all welcomed her with open arms. She should probably speak.

Abigail stood. She steepled her hands together before realizing how nervous she was and placed them at her side. "Thank you, each and every one of you to welcome me with such open arms. I do, however, have one request."

"Oh?" her husband asked, his eyes amused.

"Yes, I'd like if you all would call me Abigail."

Nora smiled. "We certainly can do that. Now, boys, it's time to clean up."

Everyone left at Nora's command while the two women cleared the dishes. Nora began to warm some fresh milk in a kettle on the stove. She reached for the cocoa and while the milk heated, measured out enough to make a large kettle of hot chocolate.

While they were inside, the others had gone to sit on the front porch. The sound of a harmonica rent the air. One of the men began to sing, then some clapping and laughing went on.

Abigail helped to hand out tin mugs filled with hot cocoa. She sipped on hers while standing beside her husband watching the day come to an end. The clouds began to fade away, while an orange glow struggled to stay in the sky as darkness descended upon the earth.

Luke said softly, "It's a clear night. I love to watch the sun go down."

Abigail agreed. "I've never seen it from this point of view. In Philadelphia there were too many buildings to stand in the way. I think I understand why people prefer to travel here. What a lovely night."

Luke nodded. "With lovely company, too."

If the sun hadn't gone down, Luke would've been able to see her blushing. The compliment was sweet. Even though everyone said Luke was grumpy and not nice, she was already seeing a different man. Why did he appear to everyone as so harsh? It was almost as if he were trying to appear one way when he actually had a heart of gold. "Thank you, Luke. That's kind of you to say so."

"Well, looks like we better get a game of cards going now or never," Rusty mentioned. He got up from the rocker on the porch to make his way across the yard towards the barn. "Who else wants in?"

The other men joined him, muttering that Rusty better not cheat this time.

Abigail smiled. "Are they always so brash?"

"Worse. They're being kind since there is a lady present."

"Two ladies. Your mother, also."

Luke rolled his eyes and laughed out loud. "My Ma has been in the middle of that poker game many times. You don't want to know the result, trust me."

"I'm calling it a night," his mother's soft voice called out. She stood at the door, smiling. "It was a pleasure to meet you, Abigail. I hope to see you again, soon."

Abigail didn't know what came over her but she gave the older woman a hug. "Thank you for making me feel welcomed." Usually, Abigail wasn't so open with strangers.

Except this new family of hers made her feel like she had known them forever.

Chapter 4

Luke had been riding the range for a few hours. He had checked each section of fencing to make sure it was still sturdy. He was on a ridge close to the Widow Young's property. He could see the white farm below, it's extensive pasture where cows grazed. Two riders stopped when they noticed Luke at the top of the ridge.

He turned away. Her twin sons would try to talk to him if they knew he was there. It was the last thing he wanted. He hadn't spoken to Widow Young or her boys since his Pa died.

No sense in reliving the past. It got him nowhere and fast. His thoughts turned to Abigail. He wondered what she was doing. Yesterday when he had come off the range, she was sitting on the front porch with his mother, hand sewing one of his shirts. He had neglected them but she found them in his bedroom, the place he hadn't slept in since she got here.

Instead, he had climbed up the ladder at the far end of the living room and bunked in the small loft there. He wasn't able to stand up but the soft mattress kept his tired bones from being too uncomfortable.

This morning before he left she had carried a basket filled with sewing items to his Ma's place and spent the afternoon with her again. At least they got along which was a good thing, wasn't it? Except for the fact in three months time, what reason was he going to give her why he and Abigail decided to annul the marriage?

In a few days time, he had gotten used to having her around. Even if he slept in an uncomfortable loft every night, hearing the sound of her voice humming first thing in the morning started to grow on him. She had coffee brewing on the stove and breakfast on the table before he woke up every single day this past week.

Her kind smile was the first thing he saw when he woke up. He saw it when he came in off the range every evening. She hadn't said much to him in days but when she smiled and looked at him with her sweet, kind eyes, he wanted to take her in his arms and kiss her.

He had to get a hold on himself. This wasn't good. Luke had to find a reason to be angry. Because kindness did no one any good. Hadn't he learned that a long time ago?

<><>

Abigail left the main house before late afternoon in order to start supper for Luke. She had been to visit his mother, enjoying the time they spent together. These last few days had been wonderful but it was time she began a routine of her own. Even if it was for only three months. She informed Nora she'd start cooking Luke's supper at night. It was nice and all helping Nora in the kitchen but she wanted to become a wife to Luke, then maybe he'd give up trying to get out of the marriage in three months.

Was it possible Luke was softening up? She noticed when he watched her at times, especially early morning when he thought she wasn't paying attention. He'd come down the ladder grumbling to himself and she'd watch how he'd stop to look at her.

At night, before she excused herself and after they had walked home from his mother's place, he'd take her hand and place a kiss there. He was a gentleman, not a grump like everyone said.

As she walked towards the cabin, Abigail noticed two riders along the fence line near the edge of their property. They were pointing towards the ground. She waved when one of the young men looked up. "Hello, there."

Both riders waved back. She was curious about her next door neighbors. Everyone in town seemed friendly enough so she figured they would be as well. She made her way towards the fence line. "I'm Luke's wife, Abigail. How do you do?"

"Hello. I'm Wesley Young and this is my brother Russell."

The two were identical twins with dark hair and broad smiles. "I'm pleased to meet you. What are you searching for?" She was curious why they were looking through the weeds and grass.

"A puppy."

"What? Oh, dear. How did a puppy get so far away?"

The two young men shrugged. Russell spoke up. "Coyote nabbed him. Carried him off by the scruff of his neck. We saw what happened and chased the coyote here. Lucky for the little fellow the coyote dropped him when we threw stones at him but the little fellow took off into these weeds and now we can't locate him."

"Let me help you look. Why was a small puppy outside by himself?"

Wesley piped up. "The mama had them in the yard so we made a shelter for her and the twelve pups. The doc had taken the mother inside the barn to examine her since she hadn't been doing so good and didn't the coyote jump in and snatch one of her pups."

Abigail spent the next hour helping to search. She found her way on the other side of the fence, digging through the tall grass and weeds. A small yelp rang out when she pushed away some wheat grass. "Well, hello there, trouble."

She scooped the yellow pup up and held it close since it was shaking like a leaf. A little tongue slaked out right before nuzzling her neck. She giggled at the puppy's touch. "You are a ball of trouble, aren't you?"

Abigail waved to the two on horseback, who had been further down the meadow searching. "I found her!"

They came high-tailing it back, relief on both their faces. Wesley dropped to the ground, holding out his arm. "Thank you, Abigail. We appreciate your help." He looked into her eyes and smiled.

Abigail stepped back. He looked familiar, as if she recognized him. "Do I know you?" she asked.

Wesley and Russell looked at each other. Then Russell prompted Wesley. "We better get going. Thanks again."

Wesley loaded up the puppy and took off across the meadow so fast Abigail had to shake her head. She hadn't missed the way the two looked at each other as if they got caught stealing cookies out of the sweets jar. She'd have to ask Luke about this. It sure seemed strange.

Abigail hurried back to the cabin, brushing off her now grass stained dress. Instead of changing, she threw an apron over top, washing her dirty hands.

An hour later, Luke was home. She felt frazzled and wanted to soak in a hot tub of water. She hoped he would help her drag the metal tub inside so she could wash up. Dragging herself through that dirty brush and tall grass today had been exhausting.

When Abigail yawned, Luke took her hand. "You seem tired tonight. Although I appreciate you wanting to start a normal routine, are you sure it isn't too much? We can always have supper at Ma's place. She doesn't mind."

"You are kind," she told him, watching his eyes flash when she told him so. He didn't like the compliment at all.

"I'm not kind, just looking out for my wife. Doing my duty as a husband. For three months," he added.

Abigail smiled. "Must you remind me this is for three months every time we discuss a subject?"

He shrugged. "It's a fact. I don't want you getting too comfortable here. In another month and a half I expect you to go to Miss Addie and let her know you want an annulment."

Abigail sighed. "Well, okay but will you please let me enjoy the time I have?"

Luke almost looked contrite. He pulled back his hand as he nodded. "I'm sorry. I will try to be kinder to you."

She patted his hand. "That's all I ask."

He nodded. "How was your day?"

"Wonderful. I helped your mother weed the flower beds and we made a few pies for Saturday night."

He smiled. "Oh? What is so special about Saturday night?"

"Well, Rusty's grand daughter is coming for an overnight visit. She's heading to Dallas to meet up with her husband, who has been working there for some time. Her and her son are moving there. So, we thought we'd make it special for them."

He reached across the table to wipe a splotch of dirt from her cheek. Abigail felt warm inside at his touch. "Looks like you've been hard at work in Ma's flower beds." She wanted to ask him about the neighbors but then he brushed a piece of hair back from her face. She looked into his eyes, shocked at the way he gazed at her.

Abigail had to change the subject. This was too dangerous to sit at the table with him. He was in a mood and she wasn't sure of his intentions. "Why are you looking at me like that?" she whispered.

He leaned forward and placed a kiss on her cheek. Abigail knew she was blushing all over. She'd bet if she stared at the looking glass in her room she'd be red from the top of her head to her neck.

" You look pretty tonight. I can't help myself."

She went to open her mouth but he placed a finger across her lips. "Don't," he said, his low tone rumbling close to her ear. His mouth covered hers in a sweet kiss that almost caused her to see stars.

"Oh," she whispered after he pulled back, his face so intense it worried her.

Luke stood. Almost as if he were mad at himself for kissing her. "I'm sorry, perhaps I was being too forward."

Abigail wanted to tell him if he wanted to kiss her again she was in agreement but sat there, dumbfounded instead. When she stared at him, he shook his head and turned towards the door.

"I'll be outside on the porch," he told her, his voice on the abrupt side.

"I'll be darned," she said aloud. Placing fingertips over her mouth, she swore she could still feel his lips there. This was the most unexpected kiss ever. Perhaps she was right, Luke was softening towards her.

The thought gave her some hope. Maybe in three months time, she'd still have a home here. Dazed, Abigail forced herself out of the chair. She took their dishes to the kitchen and began to warm up the pot for cocoa. After several minutes and hoping it was enough time that Luke was over his tempting ways, she placed their cups on a tray and went outside.

"Thanks," he told her, still not looking in her eyes. They sat side by side on the rockers on the front porch, the skyline fading fast.

"You're welcome." Their words were stifled. Abigail didn't know what to say. This was awkward.

"Looks like a full moon tonight," he mentioned.

Abigail hated small talk. She turned to Luke. Placing a hand on his forearm, he stiffened at her touch. She almost pulled back but left her hand lingering there instead. He was giving her mixed emotions and she had enough. "We need to talk."

He shrugged. "Not much to talk about." He took a sip of the hot cocoa, making it a point to stare into the cup as if the liquid was the most important thing at the moment.

"Luke White, please put that cup down and look at me." Her voice held enough emotion Luke did as he was told, which surprised Abigail.

"So talk."

"You don't have to be so mean, Luke."

"I'm not mean. The kiss happened. It meant nothing."

Abigail was shocked he would say such words. Was this the angry, mean Luke she had heard so much about? "How can you say it meant nothing? I know I felt something and I believe you did, too."

He shrugged. "A man has needs. That's all."

Abigail stood. She turned to face him, her temper at a boiling point. He was not going to get away with this, not if it were up to her! "Luke White, I've had enough of you and your asinine thinking."

He looked taken back when she swore. Slowly, he came up off the chair to stand in front of her. "I'm telling you the truth, it was a mistake. We can't do this. In three months, you'll be well on your way to marry someone else. It has to be this way."

She stood there, hands fisted on her hips. The darkening sky placed shadows across his face, it was hard to see his emotions so she took a step closer. She wanted to look into his eyes.

"I asked you to let me at least enjoy this time and now you've ruined all of it, every single second! I don't believe that you took a kiss like the one we shared so lightly. I'm sorry, Luke, but I know you have a soft, good heart and yet you hold back when it comes to us. I just haven't figured out why you are afraid to show me you care!"

She was about to stomp off when she turned back around and took his face in the palms of her hands. She stood on her tiptoes and laid the biggest kiss on him, then pulled away and stomped inside, slamming the door. Her heart fluttered so loud she wondered if he heard it through the thick wooden door.

"I can't believe I did that!" Her fingers went to her mouth and she giggled. He had made her so mad she lost her temper and acted like a saloon girl. If anyone saw her now, they'd never speak to her in public again. For once, she was glad to be away from the big city. If she had acted this way in Philadelphia, she would be labelled a brazen woman.

It took awhile for Abigail to catch her breath. She heard his boots click across the porch and then the sound faded away. Had he gone to his mothers? She peeked out the window but didn't see him. Perhaps he was fetching the buggy to take her back to Wichita Falls right now.

Oh dear, what should she do? Go after him? That hardly seemed to work. She had tried to confront him about his feelings and look what happened? Abigail paced back and forth. She needed to apologize but the look on his face when she kissed him had made her realize he did care. There was a reason he didn't want to get too involved, but why?

He loved his mother. All three of the boys did. It was because of her that he agreed to marry a mail-order bride. There was something going on that didn't make sense. Maybe Nora would know. Except she didn't dare speak to her about the two of them, otherwise she'd know her son never intended to go through with the marriage contract.

Abigail was frustrated. She stopped to stare out the kitchen window but there were no signs of Luke, not even a shadow crossing the yard.

It was better to end this night, she mused. Abigail finished cleaning the kitchen and doused the oil lamp hanging on the hook on the wall in the living room. She left a light burn on the kitchen table, so it wouldn't be completely dark when he returned. Retreating to her bedroom, Abigail crawled under the covers, the sound of the quiet night keeping her from sleep. It was going to be a long night.

Chapter 5

Luke knew he messed up. Bad. He had kissed her without thinking of the consequences. But all he could think about was having her lips on his. She was beautiful, kind, loving and Luke was honestly afraid this woman had the ability to melt his cold heart.

He honestly didn't think she would have this kind of effect on him. He thought he had it all figured out, how he'd put up with a mail-order bride for the next three months to appease his Ma and then send her off with a better deal than she had bargained for.

He even tried to tell himself the kiss meant nothing. Tried to tell Abigail too but she refused to accept his lies. And that's what they were, lies. He wanted her kisses more than anything. Every single time he looked into her eyes he ached to hold her in his arms.

This was so unexpected. Luke grinned. She sure put a kiss smack dab on him as if to say, how do you like that! He loved her spunk. At all costs, she had to believe he didn't care enough to keep her on as his wife. How was he going to do that when every time they were together he wanted to kiss her? Yet, he knew better, this was not going to be anything more than a three month arrangement. It was important for her to leave when the time came. The thought saddened him immensely. He was getting used to having Abigail around.

Luke wasn't about to be the one to unravel everything the three of them had kept quiet about for the last ten years. It would break his Ma's heart.

He wasn't willing to break her heart. Maybe he needed to talk to his brothers. Luke headed across the meadow towards the stables where his brothers would be knee deep in a card game. He was softening up and he had to be hard and cold about this whole situation. Maybe they'd knock some sense into him.

When Luke entered, Samuel was laughing so hard he almost knocked down the small table they had set up for a card game. Adam was the quiet one, concentrating on his hand. His brothers liked to compete against each other. He watched as Samuel tried hard to distract his brother but Adam was a fierce rival. Adam kept a poker face until the card reveal.

Of course, Luke knew Adam would win. He usually always did. Samuel didn't take the game as serious as his brother so it was almost a daily occurrence when he lost. He was more about having fun than anything.

Luke loved his brothers with his whole heart. He remembered how the three of them held each other up when his father passed away. How they vowed to take care of Ma and to keep their Pa's secret no matter what.

A heavy burden had fallen upon him the day he found out about the secret. His brothers knew the whole story but it was up to him to make sure they all followed his path. He was the oldest, he had to set an example for the rest.

Samuel whistled. "Well, well, well. Look who is out and about after supper. What's wrong, brother, are you tired of married life already?"

Luke glared. "Not now, Sam."

Adam jumped in. He had always been the peacemaker of the family. "That's enough, Sam. Doesn't look like Luke wants to hear any of your teasing right now."

Samuel closed his mouth. There was a time for fooling around and a time for seriousness. The rest of the ranch hands threw their cards in the pile.

They filed out one by one, grumbling how Adam always won the pot. It was the same old story every night. Except when Luke played. He usually beat Adam by a long shot. Luke grinned. He was the only one who could.

When the three of them were the only ones left in the barn Luke sat down with the others.

"What's going on, Luke?" Adam was always good at knowing when Luke was stressed out. "You having marriage issues?"

Luke propped his elbows on his knees. "You know darn well this marriage is a farce. I'm doing it to appease Ma and both of you may have to do the same thing if this doesn't work out on my end."

"Why wouldn't it work out? I have no intention of getting hitched," Adam told him. "Not one bit. You said she'd be ready and willing to high-tail it out of here in a month or two. You promised us we didn't have to go through with any fake marriages, that you'd be the one to steer the woman away. You said after you were done, Ma wouldn't try to marry us off! I remember every single word."

Luke sighed. "So I thought. Abigail is not so easy to scare off. This woman stands toe to toe with me, I can't make heads or tails of this relationship."

Adam ran a hand over the small whiskers on his chin. He didn't like to shave except when he was prompted to look his best for Sunday church services. "I kind of like Abigail. She helps Ma out a lot. Every day they spend time together so Ma isn't so lonely. Why not keep her for Ma?"

Samuel nodded. "We should do that. Ma's never been so happy as when Abigail shows up each morning."

"Samuel! Adam! You know we can't do this. We made a vow. Ma can never find out the truth, it will devastate everything she has worked for. Keeping this family small will ensure Ma never knows."

Adam struggled to keep still. "I may want to marry someday. Abigail is nice and I like having a woman around the place, besides it does make Ma happy. Isn't that what we wanted, to keep Ma happy?"

"The only way you can marry is if you leave the ranch. Are you willing to give all this up? Because it is the only way." Luke stared at his brother. Why hadn't Luke realized bringing a woman here would make his brothers long for something different? If it came down to a choice, he'd rather see Adam far away from home and happy than have Ma find out the truth.

Samuel piped in, a grin on his face. "Adam is too darn ugly to find himself a woman."

Adam stood up, his face serious. Or, so they thought. He leaped across the table, landing dead on his younger brother. Luke shook his head and laughed. He guessed their talk was over.

The two tumbled around the barn like a bunch of teenagers even though they were well into their early twenties.

"Promise me one thing, brothers?"

Adam and Samuel looked up from their wrestling. "What?" They both spoke at the same time.

"That no matter what, no matter how much I may start to care, remind me Abigail can't stay. We made a promise."

His reluctant brothers agreed.

Luke felt as if a heavy burden had planted itself on his shoulders. It had been placed there ten years ago. Except now, he had to keep up the farce, take care of his Ma and hope and pray to God she never became suspicious.

It was important that no matter the cost, Ma was never to find out the hidden truth.

<><>

"Abigail, would you mind taking a basket to the orchard for some more apples? I think apple dumplings on the menu tonight will make everyone happy."

Abigail picked up the basket. "Anything you make for these men will make them happy. They all eat as if they are starving."

Nora laughed out loud. "That's my boys."

An approaching buggy was making its way down the lane. The women went out on the porch to greet the visitors.

"Miss Nora! Hello!"

Rusty's grand daughter waved from a buggy that was filled to the brim with carpet bags, furniture and what-not. The one side tilted dangerously low.

Nora waved. "Come on in, Melody! Bring the little one, too." Abigail searched the clutter for a child but didn't see anyone at first. All of a sudden a head popped out of the mess.

Bright red curly hair surrounded a chubby face sprinkled with freckles. The little boy smiled shyly.

"Say hello, Tommy."

He lifted a toddler sized hand and waved at the women. The boy crawled over top some of the supplies on board, then slid his chubby little form down over the side of the buggy. After plopping to the ground, he got up, swiped at his knees and followed his mother to the porch.

Abigail wondered what it would be like to chase a little one around like him. An ache stirred in her heart knowing it would never happen. Not here anyway, not unless Luke changed his mind about their marriage.

When he had come home the other night, he went directly to his loft and hadn't said much since. In the morning, he no longer lingered while she made breakfast but ate quickly and left before they were even able to start a conversation.

Abigail felt the loss. She hadn't realized how powerful her kiss had been. Maybe she needed to talk to him, apologize for taking it upon herself to kiss him that way.

A tug on her dress caught her attention.

"Hello, Tommy. What is it?" His head was thrown back. A thick neck stretched to look up at her.

"Can I help pick apples?"

She didn't realize she was still holding the basket to pick apples in. Thoughts of Luke had distracted her again. "Why, of course, Tommy. Let's pick a whole bunch so we can make delicious dumplings tonight for dinner and then I bet you would like to eat a fresh, delicious one right now!"

"Oh yes, I would!" He grabbed her hand. It was sticky but warm. The two of them hurried to the apple orchard which sat a ways from the house.

Tommy had been walking so fast she was barely able to keep up. "Slow down."

He looked at her, his face serious. "It's important we get to the apples before the worms do. My momma says for me to eat my apple every day or the worms will eat it first."

Abigail held back a laugh. "I don't think there are any worms here right now. Let's take a look."

They both got busy deciding on the best of the fruit from the tree, making sure no worms infiltrated when a rider stopped. Abigail held her breath when she saw it was Luke.

The little boy turned. He began to jump up and down. "Luke! Hello, Luke! Can I go for a ride now? Please?"

The smile on Luke's face was incredible. "Sure thing, little buddy. Are you finished picking apples?"

Tommy put the two apples he held into the basket. "Yes, I am."

He ran over to Luke who helped him onto the saddle. Abigail watched in amusement as little Tommy abandoned her for a ride on a horse.

Then Luke looked at her. The man was charming, especially when there was a little boy involved. Her heart dropped four feet to the bottom of her boots when he gave her a smile and wink and rode off.

How was Abigail going to get through the rest of the day after that?

"Hello, I'm Melody. It looks like you lost your little helper."

Abigail smiled. "I believe a horsey ride is much more adventurous than picking apples."

"Don't you worry, I'll help. I was happy to hear Luke finally took the plunge and got himself a wife. Welcome to the ranch. My grandpa has been a part of this place for many years."

"Hello. It's nice to talk to someone who is familiar with this place." She didn't mention aloud that she was anxious to hear what Melody had to say about Luke since Melody had known him for a long time.

Melody shrugged. "We stayed here many times over the years. My folks wanted me to have a broader horizon. They said it didn't hurt to learn how a ranch worked since we lived in the city. Honestly, I think they just liked getting away from the busy city themselves."

Abigail observed Melody. She was younger and seemed so happy. "How long are you staying?"

Melody twirled around in a circle and giggled. "Just until Sunday. I used to do this every time I was sent for apples. One time Miss Nora thought I got lost but she found me here pretending to be dancing with my darling. Now, I am happily married and can't wait to get to Dallas so we can dance some more."

"How long have the two of you been apart?"

"Not long, a few months at the most, but its been awful. When his company moved him I stayed behind to pack and sell the items we won't be needing in Dallas." Her eyes lit up when she spoke of her husband.

"You must love him very much."

Melody had stars in her eyes. "Oh, I do! He is my everything. Well, you should know the feeling, being married to such a wonderful man as Luke."

"I have to be honest. I'm a mail order bride."

Melody swung around with a huge smile. "You are? How intriguing!" She took a step closer, observing Abigail more closely. "Why, I've never met one until now!"

"I've never been one until now!" Abigail replied.

They both laughed. "Come on," Melody told her. "Let's help make these apple dumplings and then we'll have some tea on the porch and you can tell me all about your mail order bride experience."

They headed back to the ranch house, arm in arm with a basket filled with apples. "I'm not sure there is much to tell."

Melody giggled. "With Luke, I'm sure there is."

The two women spent the afternoon alongside Nora baking apple dumplings. The smell inside the ranch house was incredible. Some of the hands wandered through, finding excuses to ask Nora questions that were meant for Luke or Adam in hopes of receiving a taste of the delectable pastries.

Nora shooed each one of them out the door with a promise of an apple dumpling for desert. Once they had her word, they were happy to oblige.

"I see this place is still like one big, happy family," Melody told Nora.

Nora sniffed. "Yes, they are all my kids if I have time to think about it. Sometimes they act like children. I have to keep each and every one of them in line. Even your grand father."

"Especially him, I'm sure!"

Nora wiped her hands on the apron. "That's all for now, ladies. I'm going to rest a might if you don't mind. Age is creeping up on me."

Abigail was right by her side. "Are you not feeling well, Nora?"

"I'm fine, trust me. Last night was difficult for me to fall asleep. It was the anniversary of my husband's death ten years ago yesterday so I didn't sleep well. Happens every year."

"I'm sorry." Abigail gave her a hug. "We'll make some tea and sit on the porch so you can get some rest. I'll keep everyone away so they don't disturb you."

Nora hugged both ladies. "I appreciate you both. Melody, I'll miss you when you are away in the big city of Dallas but remember you always have a home here if you need one."

When Nora went to her bedroom, Melody frowned. "I wonder why she said that?"

Abigail carried a tray with two cups of tea outside while Melody followed. She sat the tray on the small table between the rockers. "I'm sure it was meant as a courtesy."

Melody chewed her bottom lip. "I wonder if my grandfather was mentioning the fact my husband hadn't wanted us to follow him to the big city at first."

"I'm not sure." Abigail sipped on her tea.

"It's true, I complained to my grandfather how unfair my husband was acting. Grandpa told me to take the bull by the horns and start packing. So, I did. When my husband came home for the weekend a month ago, I gave him four weeks to find us a new home in Dallas. What you see in that buggy is all of our possessions."

"Good for you. I'm certain he will be so happy to see you made the move."

Melody shrugged. "He doesn't exactly know *when* I'm coming. I told him four weeks but yesterday I got a telegram from Dallas telling me he hadn't found a big enough place yet. You see, he is staying at one of the city's premier hotels and his company is paying for the room and may not agree to have us there. It's too late now, I've already made the arrangements and sold most of our belongings."

Abigail became worried. "He doesn't know you are coming?"

She shook her head. "I'm afraid not. But the suite he described where he is staying should be plenty big enough until I can help secure a place of our own. He needs me more than ever. He said he is so busy he hadn't had time to rent anything. I hope I'm doing the right thing."

Abigail patted her hand. "I'm sure he will be ecstatic to see you and Tommy."

Melody smiled and sighed. "I'm sure, too. He loves when I take matters into my own hands."

Abigail wanted to broach the subject of Luke. She tried to be nonchalant. "So, you have known Luke all of your life?"

Melody placed her tea cup back on the tray and took Abigail's hand. "Yes, since I was about three years old when we'd come to visit Grandpa every summer. Luke is a little older so I didn't spend much time with him but he was always so serious. Now, Adam, he's my best friend. We spent all of our time together climbing trees and swimming in the water hole on the property. Samuel would tag behind. Sometimes we'd let him come along but he was so annoying."

Abigail frowned. "Luke is different when we are alone. Everyone thinks he is so cold and serious. I see another side of him. At least I did until the other night."

"What do you mean? Did something happen?"

Abigail nodded. "I answered the ad as a mail order bride because I wasn't about to marry the man my parents wanted me to. He was old and scary. When I got here, Luke told me upfront he was marrying me to appease Nora, who was insisting all her sons find brides before she gets too old. He has it all figured out. In the contract from Miss Addie it clearly states in three months if we are not happy, Luke can annul the marriage."

Melody's eyes got huge. "He did what! Oh, wait until I speak to him!"

"Oh, no, please. You can't say a word. Nora is not to find out. I promised."

"What exactly did you promise?"

"That I'd never mention the terms of agreement to Nora. In two months, I'll go see Miss Addie and announce the marriage isn't working and she'll send me on my way as a mail order bride somewhere else."

Melody crossed her arms across her ample front. "Now that makes no sense. I saw the way Luke was watching you when he picked up Tommy at the orchard. There is something more to this story than meets the eye."

"I get the same feeling."

Melody turned to her, a look of surprise on her face. "I know what to do! It's so easy! An annulment is for couples who have not met in the marriage bed."

Abigail was starting to follow her meaning. Her eyes widened at the brashness of Melody's statement. "I, yes, you are correct."

Melody stood and placed two hands on her hips. "Well, then, darling, you better get busy and become his wife in more ways than one. If that's the case, he can't send you away."

Abigail stood too, quite shocked. "How in the world will I do that?"

Melody laughed. "Oh, darling, it won't be difficult at all. Take it from a married woman, I'll give you all the details after we settle Tommy for his afternoon nap."

Abigail wasn't sure if she should be shocked or excited to learn how to seduce her own husband. Will this work? Can she keep herself from leaving here and secure a place on the White Ranch after all?

Chapter 6

Abigail, Melody and Nora handed each man a dumpling as Rusty sat on a stool in the yard and played his fiddle. Some of the hands sang along to the music. It was a warm September evening as everyone gathered around the front porch, some men leaning against the rails while others sat on the steps or mingled in the yard.

Abigail handed Luke an apple dumpling before sitting beside him on a bench pushed up against the wall on the front porch. He had slid over when he saw her coming. When their hands touched, sparks flew up her arm. She blinked, shocked that his touch got to her so fast. How was she going to follow Melody's instructions if he made her feel out of control whenever their skin touched?

Luke didn't speak much while he ate his dumpling besides a moan here and there. Abigail looked at the others and they were all doing the same thing. Even the fiddle became silent as Rusty gobbled his apple dumpling down.

Melody sat on the step with Adam, leaning her head on his shoulder. She had mentioned they were best friends. Yet, there was a spark in Adam's eye she wondered if Melody was aware of. It was plain to see from Abigail's perspective.

"I'll miss Melody when she leaves tomorrow." Abigail had enjoyed her company, even the conversation they had earlier in secret on how to take matters into her own hands.

Luke nodded. "I'm sure you will. She's been a staple of this family since I can remember. Every summer her parents came here to get out of the city until they retired some time ago. They moved to Montana from what I understand."

"She told me all about it. I'm worried for her though. Her husband doesn't seem too fond of her moving to the big city. He had wanted her to stay behind because he hadn't found a home yet. Melody and Tommy are going to surprise him."

Luke didn't say anything for some time, instead, he stared at Rusty playing the fiddle. It was a lively tune which got some of the ranch hands stomping their boots and slapping thighs. He turned to her, staring into her eyes. "I'll talk to Adam. They're best friends."

"Want to dance?" Abigail asked, ready to start charming her husband like Melody had instructed earlier. Melody said to get close to him as much as possible and he wouldn't be able to resist her.

Was she ready to chance making him her husband for all time? Abigail didn't want to be thrown to the side by Luke and forced to start all over. She liked it here. Nora had taken her under wing and made her feel welcome. Even Samuel and Adam treated her like a sister.

Why would she want to start over somewhere else? Besides, it would break her heart to leave Luke now. Determined to make him see the error of his ways, she stood, not giving him a choice.

Luke followed suit, taking her arm as he led her to the yard. Two of the ranch hands were kidding around, dancing together as a couple. The others were laughing and teasing them while Luke and Abigail fell into the shadows.

Luke's arms around her waist made her gasp at first. Then she found the warmth of them as she allowed herself to move closer. She raised her hands to his shoulders, resting her fingertips on his strong muscles.

He nuzzled his cheek against hers. "I should steer clear of you."

"Why?" she whispered. She desperately wanted to place her lips against his skin but was worried he would figure out she was trying to seduce him. Melody said it had to look natural, as if they both were in need of each other.

Abigail was scared to death he would react in a negative way and brush her aside. She closed her eyes, allowing the sway of his hips to lead them in a dance across the yard. A fiddle played somewhere far away, it's fading music no longer needed as they stepped together in unison to the sway of each others bodies. Voices, laughter and words hung way back in the recess of her mind as Abigail boldly pushed herself closer.

She was going to become his wife tonight.

It was bound to happen sooner or later and the sooner the better.

Luke kept moving them both in the direction of the barn. Abigail nestled against him now, not caring if anyone looked up and saw them. She raised her face to touch his mouth with her own. The instant she did so, his arms closed in tighter. He was so strong it almost took her breath away. She pulled back to stare into his eyes. Even in the darkness she saw his need for her.

When his mouth touched hers again it was good he had his arms wrapped around her. His mouth lingered over her own as he pulled her closer. Their bodies were plush against each other. A need began in her belly, a feeling of being powerless while in his arms.

Wasn't she the one who was supposed to seduce him? Why was she unable to move, to do nothing but feel how his touch made her surrender?

The gentle neigh of a horse echoed in her head but she was too far gone to realize she was in the barn. Coarse strands of straw pushed against her skirt as she leaned against a bale of hay. She clung onto Luke's strong arms as his breathing became heavier.

"I can't stop myself," Luke told her, his voice a ragged whisper. "Tell me to stop, please," he begged her, his warm breath in her ear.

Abigail placed the palms of her hands against his cheeks. She was surprised at the strong protective feelings she had for him. "I can't stop you. I don't want to," she told him, her raspy voice barely above a whisper.

He groaned and kissed her again. Abigail was barely able to think. Yet, she knew if she made him her true husband this way, the guilt would overcome and she'd never forgive herself. Oh, why a conscience now?

"Luke, stop."

He paused. His arms loosened at once. They left her and hung by his side. "I'm so sorry, Abigail, did I hurt you?"

She shook her head back and forth. "No, Luke." Her hands still cupped his face.

He closed his eyes. "I am so sorry. I'm not sure what came over me. Forgive me."

"There's nothing to forgive." Was she going to tell him that she was the one to entice him because she didn't want to annul the marriage in a few months? If she hadn't asked him to dance and then press against him they would not be in this position right now.

He took a step back, as if she were a wild animal ready to pounce on him. "I get near you and this always happens. You are a witch, aren't you?"

Abigail didn't know if she should cry or laugh. "A witch? Do you think I cast a spell on you, Luke? How can you say such things?"

He glared. "I'm sure you are. I told you how it was going to be. We are married in name only. Except every time I get close to you, this happens." He spread out his arms.

"Oh, Luke, I'm not a witch." Didn't he know they had mutual feelings for each other and his plan was starting to backfire on him? How was she going to convince him?

The anger that flashed in his eyes worried Abigail. She moved towards him but he stepped back as if she were going to devour him. "Did you do this on purpose? Lure me here to make sure we?" He left the sentence unfinished. Her hand went to her mouth. How dare he once again accuse her of, of, what? Seducing him? Because it was true, that's exactly what she had been doing.

She stood her ground. Hands fell to her hips. "Yes, I did." Abigail took a step towards him. It was now or never. She was going to give everything she got to this man and if he still refused then she would be on her way sooner than later.

He backed away. "What are you doing, Abigail?"

"Luke White, it's true. Maybe I am a witch after all. Except the plain truth is yes, I was trying to seduce you into the marriage bed. I will not give up until I succeed so you better stay far away or you will wind up there, I promise you this."

He was near the entrance to the barn, his eyes popped open wide. "What the-"

She kept moving until he was through the door. She followed him outside. "I won't stop now, Luke. I didn't come all this way to be refuted like an ugly swan. If you step one foot inside our home, be prepared, Mr. White. Because I'm going to make you mine no matter what!" She was shouting now, her finger poking into his chest.

The fiddle had stopped as the others turned to the two standing outside the barn. A silence so loud covered the yard.

Abigail was afraid to look up to see if his mother watched. She didn't want to know if they had heard her words. Embarrassed, she lifted her skirts and marched away towards their little cabin down near the edge of the property.

She spun around one last time to find he hadn't moved from where she left him. The others in the yard were slowly dispersing, stretching their necks to see what else happened. Abigail didn't see Nora anywhere. The only two in the yard were Luke's brother and Melody as they talked, oblivious to what was going on around them.

Luke turned away from her towards the house. He looked back one last time then went inside, closing the door behind him.

A tear ran down Abigail's cheek. She hadn't meant a word of what she said to him. She wasn't about to seduce her husband. What in the world made her say all that nonsense? Melody had given her courage earlier that day but there was only so much seducing a woman can do until she realizes the man doesn't want her.

"It looks like no matter what I say or do he doesn't want me," she cried out, realizing how awful she may have sounded. How did she let her emotions get the best of her?

Abigail sat down on the rocker on the porch realizing any man would kiss her like that if she tried to seduce them. It was her idea to dance in the first place. Wouldn't any other man have done the same thing?

Except Luke wasn't any other man. He was her temporary husband. The man she'd be leaving in another month and a half. Perhaps she should leave tomorrow, get the waiting over with. There was no sense in pretending this was a real marriage even if she made a bargain with him. Her emotions were out of control at this point and she needed to sleep on things before making a rash decision. No one said it would be easy to pull this off.

Abigail let the tears fall. Maybe a good cry was all she needed. When she lifted her head ten minutes later, the sky was littered with tiny stars as far as the eye could see. It was a beautiful, clear night. She wanted to spend it with Luke but here she was, alone.

He had chosen his mother's house instead of coming home to discuss the two of them.

She stood and stared up at the sky. "Oh, tiny stars, if only you could make my wishes and dreams come true." There were no shooting stars she could wish upon tonight.

"Abigail." His voice was low, his steps sure as he came across the yard.

He had come back after all. She looked up at the stars, giving them a small smile. Maybe someone up there heard her cries after all.

She stood there, watching him and then he was in front of her. "I'm sorry."

Her cheeks, still wet from the tears made her shiver. "I,"

He placed a finger over her mouth. "No, please, let's not talk. Come, sit down with me."

They sat, rocking back and forth, not saying a word at first. He took her hand in his as if it were the most natural thing to do.

"Why did you come back?"

"Ma kicked me out of the house."

Abigail grinned. She flung back her head and let out a slow laugh. Luke joined in, shaking his head.

Abigail closed her eyes and rocked back and forth. "I love your mother."

"I know you do and you treat her well. Just like a daughter would." She smiled at his words.

"Let's call a truce tonight, shall we?"

His warm hand still held hers. She liked this side of him. "OK, lets. I'm sorry I seduced you."

He squeezed her hand. "I'm not."

Chapter 7

Abigail waved to the others as they rode away, heading to Dallas. Melody had been so excited to be on her way. Rusty and Adam decided to follow along, mainly to make sure Melody didn't run into any problems. Someone had spent time rearranging the buggy so all of the furniture and bags fit. It was no longer leaning to one side. She had a sneaking suspicion it had been Adam.

Nora and two of the ranch hands had decided to take a trip to Wichita Falls for one reason or another so Abigail was left to her own means today. Luke had already gone with Samuel and the others out on the range which meant he wouldn't be home until well after supper time.

She decided to pick some apples to make a few pies. It would keep her busy most of the day. Abigail went inside Nora's house to find a basket and then made her way to the orchard. After gathering what she needed, she began the long trek back to their cabin, glad for the long walk. It was a beautiful fall day even though the temperature didn't change much here. Not like in Philadelphia. There, the seasons changed. By this time of year, a light shawl had to be worn when outside. Here, the weather was nice, almost perfect. Like her life right now.

She didn't want to think of the future. For now they had called a truce. Luke hadn't said anything more of future plans or whether he'd thought about not sending her back. Last night on the porch watching the stars with him had been so wonderful compared to earlier that night when she had tried to seduce him.

It had been nice to sit and stargaze while he told her stories of how his brothers always got the three of them in trouble over the years. Abigail had laughed long into the night until Luke warned her they'd have a hard time getting up if they didn't retire.

He had left her at the door of her bedroom, kissing her lightly on the cheek like any gentleman would have done. "I promise we will discuss our situation but not now. I refuse to ruin our evening."

She hadn't said a word. It wasn't because she didn't have anything to say. She was unable to. Her throat had been choked up with tears of joy at his words.

Perhaps he was willing to change his mind after all.

Only time will tell, she had thought last night. Abigail had lain awake, staring out the window at the clusters of stars, wondering how her life was going to turn out. Her last thoughts before she drifted off were if dreams did come true when wishing upon a star, she had plenty of them to wish upon.

A movement in the distance distracted her thoughts. Over the fence line, a furry little ball of golden honey frolicked in the tall grass. She hurried towards the familiar pup, the one she called Trouble, shocked he had gotten so far from home again. Abigail's heart began to hammer. She prayed a coyote wasn't chasing him.

Abigail tried to lean over the fence but wasn't able to reach him. He jumped around like a little rabbit instead of a puppy as she stretched her hand to no avail. Finally, after looking to make sure there was no one on the range watching, she hiked up her skirts and carefully jumped the fence.

Abigail jumped when a portion of her skirt got caught on the ragged wire. She yanked hard at the cloth once she was over the fence only to hear it tear off, leaving a large patch behind. She grimaced, then left the patch there since the puppy began to run through the tall grass.

"Trouble! Come here, pup, come on!" She had left the basket of apples on the ground on the other side of the fence except for two in her pocket. Pulling out the juicy apple, she hoped it was enough to lure the puppy out of the grass.

Hours later, she looked back, unable to see the cabin. Abigail hadn't realized she had walked so far. The pup kept moving along, it's chubby behind sticking out from the grass enough so Abigail was able to follow along but he darted back when Abigail tried to snatch him up.

Frustrated, she pushed the loose strands of hair from her eyes. It was getting later and later but there was no way she'd leave little Trouble out here with coyotes and bears. Abigail's fears came to fruition. Were there bears in Texas? She shivered at the thought, realizing she was out on the prairie with no means of protection.

The moment she contemplated retracing her steps the little fur ball darted out of the grass to hide under her skirts. Abigail squealed with delight. Exhausted, she reached down and scooped the little pup into her arms. "You are very, very bad," she scolded, running a hand over Trouble's yellow head. "Why in the world do you keep leaving your home to come all the way out here?"

The pup sniffed at her before curling deep in her arms. A sense of protectiveness washed over Abigail as she realized the pup was content to be held. "You must be exhausted, too. Let's sit here and rest for a few minutes before trying to find our way back." Abigail found a tree limb lying on the ground beside a large trunk. She settled on the ground, leaning against the limb and cuddled the pup in her arms. Abigail pulled an apple from her pocket.

She began to rock little Trouble back and forth. Taking a bite of the apple, the pup lifted its head and sniffed at the fruit. She bit a piece off, handing it to him but he buried his head in her lap and fell asleep.

Abigail finished her apple, wiped her mouth with one hand and laid her head back against the tree limb. She'd rest here for a few more minutes then try to find her way back to the cabin. There was still apple pies to make.

Closing her eyes, she wondered how she'd get the pup back to its owners, although if they were keeping an eye on Trouble, they'd know by now he had run off. It would be nice if the Young brothers found both of them since she figured she was as lost as the pup.

<> <>

Luke rode in from the range along with Samuel and a few of the ranch hands. They'd been checking the fences and making sure the cattle were good. Each day he sent out riders to each part of the property, meeting up at one vantage point before all riding back together.

He was hungry and ready to call it a day.

"It doesn't look like Ma and Rusty are back yet. Guess I'll head to the barn. Anyone want to join me in a game?"

A few of the other ranch hands nodded. Samuel turned to Luke. "Wonder if Abigail is making supper since Ma isn't home?"

Luke shrugged. "Probably cooking at the cabin. I'll check and let you know what time supper is done."

The others agreed heartily, grumbling about how hungry they were. "If you don't stop complaining, you can all fend for yourselves."

Luke grinned as he rode off towards home, his last remark causing havoc amongst the others. The men did deserve a hot meal after a long day on the range and his Ma always made sure they got one. If Ma knew she was going to be late, she'd have told Abigail to do the cooking or prepared something ahead of time. He hoped Ma talked to Abigail and she made enough for all the others. If not, he'd have to explain to her when Ma was away, she had to take over.

The thought occurred to him that when she left after her three months were up there would be no woman to take over for Ma the few times she was gone. It did make Ma's life easier to have someone to do the cooking when she wasn't able to and it gave her a much needed break.

It saddened him yet he was still determined his Pa's secret would never be revealed. If he let her stay, the others would want the same thing. The possibility of having the secret revealed was too great. The less people who lived on the ranch would assure them Pa's secret would stay where it belonged. He loved his Ma too much to hurt her and it would devastate her, he knew. They all knew.

The sun was starting to line itself against the horizon, causing shadows across the prairie. Luke frowned when he saw no lights inside. Why was she in the dark? A growing, nagging feeling began to rest in his stomach. If Abigail wasn't inside, where was she?

His gaze went from the cabin to the surrounding area to the ranch beyond the property line. Small dots of light protruded from far away. The Youngs were settling in for the evening after a long day on their ranch as well. Mrs. Young was probably feeding her boys right now, along with the two other ranch hands they hired. Their property wasn't large at all but it butted up against the White Ranch. It didn't take no more than three or four men to run the place.

Luke went inside the cabin. Abigail was nowhere to be found. He looked around the cabin, walked to the small stream running through the area and began to trust his intuition as he got back on his horse. He rode through the yard towards the property line. The first thing he noticed was his Ma's basket filled with apples lying on the ground beside the fence. He looked closer.

Luke leaned over to pluck the piece of fabric from the fence. "Abigail! Abigail!" He raised his voice again and again to no avail. Luke turned back and rode towards the barn. "Samuel! Get out here!"

Samuel and two of the ranch hands ran out of the barn so fast he had to pull back on the reins so quick the horse came to a complete stop about two inches from where Samuel stood. "Saddle up, I think Abigail went exploring beyond the fence."

Samuel's eyes widened. "You think she's lost?"

"I don't know but we need to find her before the Young brothers do. They see someone wandering across their property they may shoot first and ask questions later. Let's get a move on!"

Luke didn't wait for the rest. He grabbed a lantern from the barn, knowing it may help to light the way if they didn't find her before the sky went completely dark. He knew the others would as well.

Galloping across the yard and meadow, Luke jumped the fence in one leap, landing on the dreaded Young property. He was well armed in case those boys came after him. Although he doubted they would even though he told them if they step foot on White property, he'd shoot them first. They told him the same before riding off.

Luke didn't want to be mean to Wesley or Russell. It wasn't their fault what had happened so long ago. It wasn't anyone's fault except his Pa's. Luke shook himself. Thinking wasn't going to get him anywhere. He had a lost wife to find. Riding along the fence line for some time didn't bring him any more clues. He felt the fabric still in his hand. It was getting darker by the minute.

The rest of the men rode up beside him. "Are you sure she came this way?" Samuel asked, his face no longer jovial. He was as concerned as the rest. Luke knew they all liked Abigail.

He nodded. "I found this caught on the fence." He held up the torn fabric. "For whatever reason, she went over the fence and she's nowhere to be found. Guess we better split up. Watch your backs, boys. Them Youngs come wandering out, their may be trouble."

One of the ranch hands spoke up. "Want me to go see if she went visiting at their ranch?"

Luke hated getting the Youngs involved. He didn't see any reason for her to walk that far from home. She never mentioned anything about them. "Not yet. Let's see if we can find her first."

Dusk happened soon after. The darkness descended upon the riders so fast, Luke began to worry. Each man lit a lantern, enabling the light to help them see and move quickly through the tall grass. Except it didn't help find Abigail. He guessed they had no choice but to check over at the Young Ranch. "Samuel, you go on over to the Youngs and see if they know anything. Take someone with you."

Luke widened the circle. He ordered two men to ride further out while he went in the opposite direction. Soon after, he heard Rusty and his Ma.

"Son, we're here to help. We followed the lanterns."

"Thanks, Ma. I'm not sure why she went over the fence. All I know is she isn't anywhere to be found."

Nora rode beside him. "I wanted to go see Miss Addie today to order another bride since Abigail has worked out so well."

"Don't do that yet, Ma."

She tilted her head. "Why not? You and Abigail seem to be settling in."

"Hardly. We've called a truce for now." He didn't want to give her too much information or reveal the fact he didn't plan on letting her stay.

"It doesn't matter. I overlooked one thing."

Luke shifted in the saddle. He'd been in it too long today. "Yeah? What did you overlook?"

"I didn't realize we had to wait three months to make sure the marriage was working. Did you know you may annul the marriage within the three month period, Luke?"

He didn't want to lie to his Ma so he said nothing. It didn't matter because she hardly noticed and kept on talking.

"I have to wait until your three months are up to order another bride. Miss Addie informed me it was written in the contract. Somehow in my rush to see you all married, I neglected to read all of the fine print."

Luke patted his Ma's hand. "It's all good, Ma. No need to worry."

She nodded, then smiled. "So you have consummated the marriage? Good. All we can do now is wait for another three weeks, four days and fifty-six hours until I can order a bride for Adam."

Luke didn't have the heart to tell his Ma the truth. Besides, it would be awkward to do so. He turned his horse towards a large pasture where he knew there was some overgrown trees. Luke knew the land like the back of his hand even though it belonged to someone else.

When he was real young, perhaps five or six, he rode this land with his Pa. They had been helping the widow since she had just lost her husband. Samuel was way too young but him and Adam would ride with their Pa daily to help round up the cattle. Pa saddled up a pony for the two. He remembered how he'd tuck Adam in front of him since he was three years younger. Adam didn't remember much but Luke did. He remembered more than he wanted to.

"Abigail! Abigail, where are you?" Nora clasped her hands together, calling out.

The rest of the men followed suit, spreading out and calling her name. A few minutes later, Samuel and the Young twins showed up.

Luke glared at the two boys. He didn't want them around, but right now needed all the man power available.

Samuel was the first to speak up. "Wesley said a week ago one of the puppies in the new litter got taken by a coyote. They followed it to the fence line where Abigail helped them capture the pup."

"We can't find the pup. Somehow it may have made its way back to the fence."

Luke barked. "How do you lose a pup?"

Nora placed a hand on his arm. "Now is not the time, Luke." She turned to the Youngs. "We need everyone to work together. I want to know there will be no problem with that."

Wesley and his brother nodded. "No, ma'am, there won't be any trouble."

"Luke? Adam? Samuel?"

"No, Ma."

"No problem."

"Luke?"

He gritted his teeth. He wanted to chase off the Youngs but when it was all said and done if they stood here arguing, Abigail may be in grave danger. They had to find her, with the twin's help. "No problem here as long as those two steer clear of me."

"Luke, I guess that's about the best you can do. Okay, boys, let's find Abigail."

Luke was amazed at his Ma's determination and fight at her age, although it didn't surprise him. She had been a fighter all her life and stepped up to the plate when their Pa died. She was born to the saddle and led the way through the dark. He rode up beside her. "Thanks for helping, Ma."

She turned to him. "I would do anything for my daughter-in-law. Now, do a bit less talking and more searching."

Luke, stunned, began to grin. His Ma was a feisty woman. Rusty found his way alongside her while he spread out in the opposite direction. No use worrying about his Ma, too. She'd be fine.

The night air was cooling the closer they got to the small creek that ran through the property. The air was damp, a few chills ran through Luke's body. The temperature always dropped at night.

The others were calling out her name to no avail.

The return silence was getting the best of him. Where was she? Luke was more alarmed then he'd ever been in his life. He slid from the saddle and began to walk along the bank of the creek, close enough so his horse was able to drink cold water to quench her thirst. His mare had been tirelessly working all day. She needed to rest.

He stood by the creek while she dipped her nose into the water. Luke looked around, seeing nothing but darkness. He held up the lantern in his hand. A small glow made a circle surrounding him.

His mare stopped drinking. Her ears perked upward. Luke laid a hand on her neck. "What is it? What do you hear?" he whispered, knowing a horse's hearing was much better than his own.

Then Luke heard the shuffling noise. A small whimper sounded from his left. Luke moved the lantern towards a tree with large fallen branches surrounding the trunk. The tree was dying, its limbs crumbling, falling off one at a time.

A crack rent the air as another limb fell to the ground alongside the others. Luke left the horse at the creek, racing to the tree. That's when he noticed a pair of ladies boots sticking out from underneath several branches. He heard a puppy whimpering, sticking its head out then disappearing from sight.

"Abigail? Are you under there?"

No answer.

"I think I found her!" He yelled at the top of his lungs so the others would hear. Luke got to work, dragging the limbs away from the tree. It seemed like forever until every single limb had been cast aside. A shaking puppy curled up in Abigail's skirts. He picked up the pup, removing her from Abigail's lap. He placed the palms of his hands on her cheeks, finding them so cold. Her clothes were wet from the stream, it's moisture drawing into the ground, causing the dampness.

"Abigail!" Wake up!"

He placed the pup onto her lap, picking Abigail up from the damp ground. She was so limp. He didn't have time to waste. The others rushed to his side when they heard him call out.

"Have you found her? Oh, dear!" Nora rushed to his side. "Adam, take her so Luke can get on his horse."

Adam did as told, then waited until Luke was astride, handing Abigail over.

Luke gathered her close, the puppy still hiding within her skirts. Luke moved as fast as possible through the meadow land, hanging onto them both, fearing the worst. He didn't want to loose Abigail.

She was starting to mean the world to him.

Chapter 8

Abigail heard the sound of Nora's voice speaking quietly to her son. She didn't want to open her eyes to let them know she was awake. Actually, she was enjoying this time, listening to his Ma reprimand her husband. She tried hard not to move a muscle so they weren't aware she was indeed awake.

"Luke White. I've never been so ashamed of one of my sons before. The way you treated the Young twins was terrible. If your father were alive, he'd have sent you to bed without food."

"I'm a grown man, Ma, no one can send me to bed without my supper."

"That doesn't mean you have to disrespect someone. Those two spent the night looking for your wife."

She heard Luke sigh. Abigail imagined he was staring at his boots right now. When Nora got mad, she didn't hold back. Even though she was whispering from a corner of the room, Abigail heard her plain as day.

"I'm sorry, OK? What do you want me to do? I feel the same way about them as before Abigail got lost. Why should it change anything?"

"You didn't have to tell them not to cross over onto our property or they'd be shot on sight!"

"They told me the same thing."

"That was ten years ago, Luke. When your father died I know they made some terrible allegations about him but none of it was true. I think it's time all of you get together and stop this neighborhood feud. There is no point to all the bad feelings."

"They accused Pa of trying to scare the widow off and then offering to buy her land. I'll never forgive them for trying to accuse a dead man of something he didn't do."

"Maybe it's time to forgive."

"You haven't spoken to Widow Young in ten years either, Ma."

"I tried. She won't speak to me," his mother said softly. "She assumes I want her land as well."

Abigail listened as the two argued quietly in the corner of the room. She no longer heard precise words as they both lowered their voices again. Abigail was certain they were trying to avoid disturbing her. Now she understood why no one ever talked about Widow Young and her boys. Luke's father wanted their land. It made sense since it was butted up to theirs. She still didn't understand why there had to be so much angst among them all. Ten years was a long time to stay angry.

Abigail flickered her eyes, trying to keep still and yet wanting the arguing to stop. Her head still ached from the tree limb that fell right on top of her, sending her reeling last night. When the limb hit her it had made her so dizzy her head began to spin right before she had fainted while holding onto the puppy for dear life. The next thing she remembered was Luke holding her tight, racing through the night on his mare, whispering in her ear to please stay alive. A small smile curved at her mouth, remembering his soft-spoken words of desperation.

Luke had said if she were to live he would keep her forever, he truly did not want an annulment. Were those the words of a man who despised her? It sounded more like they were from someone who loved her. How had it happened so fast?

Abigail didn't want to face reality yet. She stayed as still as possible while the two finished their conversation. She rather enjoyed how Luke had sat by her side through the night, stroking her hand, running his fingers down her face, telling her she meant the world to him. She secretly wondered how long she would be able to stay like this? If she were to keep getting this type of attention, she may not want to awaken until Spring. By then the three month trial period would be long gone.

Abigail felt a pair of lips press against her forehead. The lavender scent she knew well from Nora lingered in the air. "I'm going to make some broth so when she wakes up it will help nourish her."

"Thank you, Ma. I'm sorry I spoke unkindly to you."

"I love you son and I do understand you have your own opinion. We'll talk about it later. Right now, we have to be here for Abigail."

Abigail almost felt a stab of guilt when she heard Nora hold back a sob.

Luke hugged her before walking her to the door. "It's going to be fine, Ma. Don't worry, Abigail is a strong woman. I felt a strong pulse, she'll wake up."

"I hope you're right. She is like a daughter to me." The front door closed quietly.

The room became unbearably silent.

Abigail opened her eyes to find Luke watching her, a smile curving his lips when he noticed she was awake. He moved closer, sitting on the chair beside the bed. Taking her hands in his own, he pressed them to his lips, his mouth lingering there. She felt the breath of warm air against her skin.

"I thought you may be awake." His quiet words made her feel even more guilty.

"I'm sorry. I didn't want your Ma to know I was awake. Or you for that matter."

"Why not?"

"All night long I heard you speaking to me. I heard what you said, Luke. I was hoping to hear more."

He sighed and looked into her eyes, his face serious. "I meant every word. I doubt I can be without you now, Abigail."

Her pulse raced at his honest words. She felt the same way. This was a dream come true, a turning point for them both. Even the pup got excited, his tiny tail pounding the blanket, making a racket.

She tried to sit up but her head began to pound. She reached for her head, hoping to make the pain go away. "Oh, my, it hurts so much."

"You got a bump the size of a goose egg on your forehead. Don't try to move. I'll take care of you."

Abigail forced a smile through the pain. "Thank you. I guess I'm fine as long as I lie still." A wet tongue slaked out, tickling her hand. Abigail giggled, grabbing her head again to still the movement.

"This little feller stayed with you the whole time. He wouldn't leave you even when I tried to give him back to the Youngs."

"His name is Trouble."

"Indeed."

Abigail wondered if he tried to give Trouble back before or after he warned them not to cross over on the White property. Now that she was staying, she began to wonder how to make everyone all get along. Maybe there was something miraculous she was able to do to bring peace to this family. It wouldn't hurt to send a small prayer upwards right now.

Twenty minutes later, the soft knock on the bedroom door sounded so loud to Abigail's tender ears. She groaned aloud in agony. The more awake and aware she became, the more pain she felt. Without a doubt she needed more rest. Except the smell of chicken broth wafted through the air. Her stomach growled.

Nora peeked her head through first before entering, the sadness no longer in her eyes. She seemed strong, pulled together, unlike earlier. "I brought some warm broth. Ah, you are awake. I knew you'd pull through." She placed a kiss on Abigail's cheek before handing the broth to her son. With a nod she left as quickly and quietly as she came.

Luke dished a spoonful and held it to her mouth. Abigail opened up, sipping on the delicious liquid. Without opening her eyes, she moaned softly. "It tastes so good, thank you so much."

"You are under strict orders to rest today. Ma sent for the doctor but the closest one is in Wichita Falls. It'll take a few hours for him to get here."

"I'm sure I'll be fine, no need to go to all that trouble."

"I'm afraid it's too late, he's sure to be on his way."

After eating half the bowl, Abigail pushed the spoon away. "That's enough. I'm getting sleepy."

Luke set the bowl aside then picked up Trouble. "I'll take him outside for a run. You get some rest. I'll bring him back soon."

"Can I keep him?" She batted her eyes on purpose even though it hurt to move them.

He grinned. "I think he's already claimed you. I'll see what I can do."

"I'm sure the Youngs won't mind if you ask nicely."

Luke frowned. "I don't plan to ask them."

Luke rode up to the front porch of the Young ranch. He hadn't been this close to the place in ten long years. The last time he remembered being on the property besides having to rescue Abigail last night was with his father. In a way the place was a tiny version of the White Ranch.

Widow Young stood on the porch, a shotgun cradled in her arms.

"Put that thing away, I'm not here to start trouble."

"Seems to me you threatened my boys again."

"Again! I'll have you know they were the ones who threatened me first."

"Humph! That was ten years ago and you deserved it acting like a darn fool."

It was a shame he had to keep this feud going for the sake of his father's secret. Luke had always liked Widow Young. She didn't mince her words. If she was mad, she let you have it. At the same time if she liked you, there was nothing she wouldn't do for you. Luke was pretty sure he was on the bad side of her, which didn't bode well with her carrying that shotgun around. It wasn't entirely her fault what had happened.

After her own husband died, she always treated Luke and his brothers with kindness. Pa, along with him and his brothers would help out whenever time allowed to keep the farm going. Even with all the work from their own farm, no one minded lending a hand for a poor widow woman.

Then something happened and it was the last time he ever got a piece of pie or sat at her table again. When she turned on them, it wasn't a good thing. He had better keep that thought in the back of his head no matter how understanding she appeared to be.

Two riders came through the pasture like they were racing the wind itself. "Get away from our Ma!"

Luke recognized Wesley's voice. He was always the loudest of the two. As protective as Luke was with his own Ma, he more than understood how Wesley felt. Still, he wasn't here to harm anyone.

"That's enough Wesley. Let the man speak."

Luke nodded to Widow Young. He reached in his pocket and handed Wesley a wad of cash. "This here's for the dog. Seems like it done got itself attached to Abigail."

Wesley glared. "Who says we are selling the pup?"

Luke moved his horse alongside Wesley. "Don't much matter to me. I figure I can keep that pup for all the trouble it caused. Because of him, my wife may have died on your property. I suggest you take the money and be darn lucky that's all I'm offering." He made a fist, clearly making a statement to the twin.

Wesley puffed up his chest. His brother sat silent, watching.

"Leave it be, son," the widow warned. She spoke to Luke. "You can have the pup, no charge. Now go on, ride out of here."

Wesley tried to hand the money back. Luke stared hard before ignoring it and moving away, backing out of the range of the Young family. He doubted they would try something but he wasn't about to turn his back on anyone. Not after everything that had happened over the years.

Once he left the Young spread, Luke shot across the open prairie giving his mare full rein. He needed to get some frustration out before going back to spend time with Abigail. Seeing the widow so close up and in that environment made him think of his father. He did miss his Pa. In ten years the ache in his heart was lighter but the anger at what his father did had grown. Luke thought it had faded but it hadn't. He'd always be angry at what the man had done, what it had cost them.

He also needed to speak with his brothers. There was so much going on in his head right now. He had made a promise, a pact with his brothers so long ago, forcing them both to promise never to reveal their secret. Under no circumstances would they ever let their Ma find out.

He knew exactly where his brothers were riding the range. He headed that way, determined to get the conversation over with. It wasn't going to be easy to admit he had been wrong.

"Luke!" Adam noticed him first. He headed towards his brothers, kicking in his heels knowing Samuel would catch up and join in. It didn't take long for all three brothers to be racing against the wind.

The adrenaline pumped through his system. This was exactly what he needed. Adam flung his head back and laughed, while Samuel, a grin on his face, leaned in to the horse, forcing it to move faster. The three men raced against each other with sheer determination. They were headed for the creek that ran through one section of the property. Luke was in the lead. It never failed, he always won.

Except today he didn't want to win. He pulled back, letting the two go ahead of him. A look of surprise rendered across Adam's face while a yippee came stumbling from Samuel's mouth. The two ran their horses into the creek at the same exact time.

"It's a tie!" Adam shouted.

"I can't believe Luke lost!" Samuel lifted his hat in the air, waving it around.

The two looked at each other for a few seconds before Luke came to a stop.

They stared at him, their faces quite serious.

Adam spoke first. "Something is wrong. You let us win."

Samuel nodded. He placed his hat back on his head, watching his oldest brother carefully.

"You are right. I let you win." Luke slid from his saddle. "We need to talk."

"Since Ma's not around, we don't need to fake a wrestling match." Adam sat down on the river bank, loosening the reins so his horse could get something to drink.

Samuel and Luke did the same.

Luke closed his eyes, listening to the running water trickle against stones and small rocks alongside the banks. The air was clear, even the birds didn't make much noise today. "I need to get some things off my chest."

"We're listening," Samuel piped up.

Adam nodded, staring at the water flowing by. To all appearances, he didn't seem to be paying attention. Luke knew better.

"For ten years we've been able to keep Pa's secret. I still plan to and I ask you both to honor that promise."

Adam frowned. "Of course we will honor it. Ma would be crushed if she found out."

Samuel agreed. "I won't ever spill my guts."

Luke sighed. "Things have changed for me and I think you both know making us swear to never marry was a foolish idea. I'll be first to apologize for holding you both to a promise I can't even keep."

Adam smiled. "You've fallen for Abigail, haven't you?" He reached out to pat Luke on the back.

Samuel brushed Adam's arm aside and pounced on his older brother. "Yahoo! I knew it!"

Luke laughed. There was no getting around it now. He'd have to fight his way out of this. Twisting his whole body, he pretended to slam Samuel to the ground, taking his arms and placing them behind his back. Samuel was no match for him, at least not yet. Maybe in a few more years he would be.

Forty minutes later they were all spread out in the grass alongside the creek bank, laughing and teasing one another. Luke sat up on his elbows. "I best get back. The doc should be here by now. I want to check on Abigail."

"Luke, with a woman like Abigail, we both knew it was a matter of time until you came to your senses. It's time you settled down and tried to forget about what happened."

Adam's words made sense, except he'd still have to keep the secret from Abigail. The less people knew about their past, the less chance of his Ma ever finding out. "I'll never forget."

"We won't either but we can't stop living."

"Or not being able to fall in love," Samuel complained.

"The less people know the better. You don't have to tell Abigail what happened."

"I don't plan to tell her right now. Maybe some day, I don't know for sure. I do know when she was lost it was hard to breathe. I tried to imagine her leaving here when I annulled our marriage. Under no circumstances will I let her become someone else's mail order bride."

Adam grinned. "Now that you made up your stubborn mind, I may as well find myself a mail order bride."

"Me, too," Samuel admitted.

"All in good time, brothers. You know Ma wants that honor."

Chapter 9

Doc James snapped his black leather bag shut. "You'll be good as new in a few days. A bump like you have will cause great harm if you don't rest and give yourself time to heal. No work, no cooking and no marital relations for a week. I think complete bed rest for a few days and then slowly get back to normal. I suppose by next Monday you'll be good as new but I'll leave a small bottle of laudanum in case you have trouble sleeping. The headaches can be awful. Use it sparingly." He handed the bottle to Nora.

A blush crawled over her skin when the doc spoke about marital relations. Abigail glanced at Nora, who turned away with a grin.

The door burst open. Luke stood there, his chest heaving. 'I'm sorry, I was out on the range. What did I miss?"

Abigail was delighted to see him. She gave him one of her best smiles. "Hello, Luke," she whispered, her head still a bit tingly from the headaches.

Luke ignored everyone and went to her side. He took both hands in his own and brought them to his mouth. "I've missed you."

Oblivious to the doctor and Nora, Abigail almost let a tear splash onto her cheek. This new, caring, loving man was making her tear up at his words and actions. Before the accident he was a decent man but very aloof. Now, he was so attentive and loving. A complete turnaround from before. She almost smiled. He had been gone all but four hours. "I've missed you, Luke."

The doc coughed.

Nora took the doctor's arm and led him out of the room, offering a slice of apple pie at her house so he wouldn't get hungry on his long trip back to Wichita Falls.

When they were alone, Luke pulled up a chair and sat there, staring.

"What? Do I look terrible?" she asked, worried the bump on her forehead made her look less appealing.

He shook his head. "You are beautiful."

Abigail let out a sigh. "A few days ago you were ready to send me on my way as a new mail order bride to a stranger when our time was up in three months. Can you blame me if I find this total turnaround absolutely fascinating albeit somewhat scary. I'm not sure I can trust your word."

"Then, let me show you." He placed a tender kiss on her lips, causing Abigail's heart to pump so fast she thought it would explode. "Luke, what happened to you?"

He released her hands and stood up, turning away at first as if it were hard to speak his true feelings. "I'm sorry for the way I behaved when you first got here and up until your accident." He swung back around, then kneeled down, taking her hands again. His emotions were all over the place but his steady gaze forced Abigail to look deep in his eyes.

"Luke, let's take this one step at a time. All I want to know is that you care about me and won't send me away at the end of the three month period. How can I trust your word?"

His hand cupped her cheek as he gazed into her eyes. "I won't ever let you go, Abigail. I was so wrong. To make up for my behavior, I'm going to court you and show you how much you mean to me. Fair enough?"

She smiled. "Court me? We are married, that may seem a bit odd to the others on the ranch. On the other hand, I do like this new behavior of yours. Fair enough, then. Now go on and let me rest. I have a lot of sleeping to catch up on."

He dipped his head and gave her a sweet kiss that made her insides tingle. When he moved away, she reached out her hand to touch his arm.

"What is it?" he instantly was back at her side, gazing into her eyes.

"Where's Trouble?"

His eyes widened. He had left the pup in the hands of Rusty while he went to the Young ranch to buy the dog. On his return he noticed Rusty heading out to one of the pastures, with no dog in hand but all Luke had cared about was getting back in time to speak with the doctor. He hadn't given the dog much more thought. "I'll be back, you get some rest."

"Luke! Luke! Why are you looking like that? Where did you leave him?"

He tried to hurry out the door. "Don't worry, everything is under control."

"Darn it, you mangy dog! Where are you?" If he didn't find the pup, Abigail would be devastated. She had put herself in harm's way for this pup and now Rusty had gone and lost him. He had searched the barn for the last twenty minutes to no avail.

Luke made his way to the main house. "Ma, where did Rusty head to?"

Nora was on the porch saying goodbye to the good doctor, who waved from his buggy. Luke waved back but his eyes were on Nora. He needed to find the pup!

Her smile turned to a frown when she saw the angry look on his face. "What's wrong? Is it Abigail? Shall we call the doctor back?"

"No, nothing like that! Rusty was supposed to watch the pup, now he's gone. I can't find him anywhere."

Nora leaned back, hands on her hips and began to laugh out loud. "Oh, I'm stunned! Just stunned!"

"What's so darned funny?"

"Come inside, Luke, the pup is fine. Come join me for a slice of apple pie."

"The pup is fine?" He crossed his arms over his broad chest.

Nora nodded. She held out her hand. "Come along, Luke, come inside and you will see I tell you the truth."

Luke followed his Ma inside like a little boy who lost his way. Nora kept laughing which made him even more frustrated. She turned to him. "You, young man, have a case of love sickness!"

"That's absurd!" Was it so easy to tell? His brothers would never let him live it down if they knew he was so scatterbrained because of a woman!

Trouble was curled near the warmth of the stove, sleeping away. Relief surged through him.

"You see," Nora told him, cutting a slice of pie, "he's perfectly fine. When will you learn to ask before jumping to conclusions? I guess in your state of mind, well, it's understandable."

Luke sat at the table, propping one elbow on the wooden edge. Even though he was a grown adult, it did feel good to sit here, one on one with the one person who loved him no matter what. She made sure him and his brothers grew up to be strong and capable men. Even though Pa was gone, she always held them together, even when things got tough the first few years. He would do anything for her, just like she'd do for all of them, and he'd keep his father's secrets from ever being brought out in the open, no matter what. He'd have to keep it from his own wife as well, even though it would be hard.

He picked up a fork and turned to the pie when his Ma set it in front of him. "Promise me you will not tell Adam or Samuel how stupid I act? They won't let me live this down. It will be horrible trying to listen to the two of them making fun of me."

Nora sat across from her son. "I believe you are being a bit dramatic, son, as usual. I promise not to mention how frantic you were trying to find the pup for the woman you love."

He set down his fork and stared at his mother in amazement. "I guess I do love Abigail." The realization hit him like a bale of hay flying across they barn yard, landing smack dab in his face.

Nora gave him her all-knowing smile that Luke knew so well. "You can thank me any time, son."

Luke grinned. "Thanks, Ma."

"You are certainly welcome. I told you I know what is good for you. Not to mention that your brothers need to follow suit. Tell me, what is the one thing I can entice Adam with in order for him to let me send for a mail order bride for him?"

Luke thought for a moment. He shook his head. "It's too late for him, Ma. Any woman will do now that the one he always wanted is married."

Nora gave him a sharp look. "Do you mean Melody? They are the best of friends, that's all."

Luke grunted, his mouth full. "Best friends? If she hadn't been so blinded by that fancy husband of hers who swept her off her feet five years ago, she'd know Adam had always been in love with her."

"Don't be ridiculous, Luke. Melody is a sweet girl, and the two have been friends since she started coming here with her parents. That's all, don't add more to it than it is."

"Well, then, I guess since he can't have Melody, he'd take a parcel of land to build himself a nice cabin like I have to bring home a bride. I doubt you will have to offer either one of my brothers anything. Now that I'm married, they will follow suit."

Nora helped herself to a slice of pie. "That's much more than a pearl-handled gun. Well, then, we best get to it since I want to see the lot of you all married by the end of the year."

"No worries here, Ma. I'll talk to him later today."

"Good."

"Ma?"

"What is it, son?"

"I want to have an outing. I guess you could call it a wedding reception."

"Oh?"

"Yes, Abigail and I got married at the church and that was the end of it. I will be honest, I didn't plan to stay married to her. In three months, when the contract is up, I had planned to send her back to Miss Addie to find her another husband."

Nora sat back, shocked at her son's words. After a few seconds, she composed herself. "You actually read the contract? Oh, dear! Did you tell Abigail this as well?"

He nodded. "I told her the day I met her. She wasn't too pleased."

"Seems your initial plans have backfired on you, son."

"Pretty well. I can't live without her now. Let me make it clear, I won't live without her, she means the world to me. I never thought I would want to feel this way about anyone. My life was perfect, or so I thought."

Nora gave the sleeping puppy a nod. "Perhaps Trouble isn't so much trouble after all."

Luke agreed. The pup was the reason his true feelings surfaced. If the pup hadn't gotten lost, he'd still be contemplating sending her back to Miss Addie. But now, things were different. As long as he kept the secret between his brothers and himself, there would be room for a wife. Why hadn't Luke seen this sooner than later? "Can you help give my wife a nice wedding reception?"

"Of course. Now, I don't want you to worry none. Go take care of your wife and I'll take care of the reception. How about two weeks from Saturday?"

Luke looked a bit sheepish. "That's the day I was going to send her away. The deadline. Now, I'm going to be throwing a big shindig to introduce the world to my wife."

Nora laughed out loud. "The world? How about a few neighbors and some members from the church, and Miss Addie herself? That's about the best we can do."

There was a small church they frequented each week about twenty minutes away from the ranch in the small rural town of River's Edge where they sometimes went to pick up certain supplies. The town was nothing like Wichita Falls or Mill Ridge and a far cry from cities like Dallas but the little town was sequestered against a ridge and running along the banks of a water supply. Hands from neighboring farms and ranches spent their Saturday nights at the saloon and dance hall, then Sunday mornings at the church on the ridge where the pastor was also the local barkeep. Didn't make much sense to Luke, but it seemed others enjoyed the place.

His Ma wasn't real crazy about listening to a barkeep preach the word of God, except for the fact Pastor Daniel did a decent job. So every Sunday morning they gathered together for the twenty minute trip to the church.

All Luke wanted now was to spend the rest of his life with his new bride, have children to carry on his name and ranch, in that order.

"Luke? Are you listening?"

"Yes, I am." Although he wasn't.

"I said we'll butcher for the meat and I'll make some side dishes to go with. Plus, you will need a wedding cake. I'll take care of that. Rusty can gather a few of his musical friends so there's dancing. I'll enjoy getting the reception ready for you and Abigail. Everyone works so hard, this will be good for the whole ranch and neighbors."

"Ma, thanks for taking care of the details. I trust your judgement."

Nora gave him a hug. "I can see your mind is on one thing right now. Here," she told him, gathering the pup from its nice, cozy spot. "Take the pup and go home. Go on, now. Take a few days off from the ranch and take care of your wife. I'll keep the boys at bay while you tend to Abigail."

"They'll have the ranch in an uproar if I let them to their own devices."

"Now, Luke, there you go being over dramatic again. The others will be fine. The ranch will be fine, good day."

His Ma turned her back to him after handing over the pup. Luke stood there for a second, holding Trouble, trying to figure out how he can walk away when the ranch needed attending to.

"Luke, I meant for you to go now. You don't have to worry about the ranch, the rest of us know how to run it without you."

"Jeez, Ma, that's harsh." He gave her a quick kiss on the cheek. "I'm leaving."

As he walked outside he heard her next words. "Thank you, God. I never thought he'd go!"

Luke made his way back to the cabin, the pup in tow. He watched the little fellow sniff around the grass, do his business then stand at Luke's feet, waiting to be picked up and carried. "I'm afraid you'll have to walk, little fellow."

Trouble gave him one of those sad, pitiful looks. Luke needed to train him to listen. "Come on," he urged and began to walk away from the pup. Except the pup got wind of the horse barn and began to head towards the noises inside.

Luke ran after him, shaking his head. Now wasn't the time to train, he imagined it would take a lot more than a gentle nudge. He scooped the dog up in his arms and went back to the cabin.

Inside, Abigail was asleep. Trouble began to wag his tail the moment he saw her lying there. "I know how you feel," he told Trouble, realizing he was discussing his feelings with a dog. His own heart pounded at the sight of his wife. Shaking his head, Luke placed the pup on the bed, where he instantly settled on Abigail's lap. He watched the two for some time before going to the kitchen to see what he could muster up for supper.

Two and a half hours later he was still sitting at the table worrying about what to cook. His Ma was adamant about him staying away from ranch work and taking care of Abigail. Luke supposed that meant doing his own cooking. He guessed he could give it a whirl.

He was also aware it would give the two of them some time together to talk. Knowing he had been a terrible husband at first, Luke was determined to make it up to her. If that was through her stomach, then he'd learn to cook somehow. Except when he looked around the stove and on the shelves for something to cook, he had no idea what to do. About the only thing he knew how to cook were eggs and beans.

Some time later, after checking on Abigail numerous times to find her sleeping peacefully, a knock to the front door had Luke quickly crossing the room. When he flung open the door, his two brothers stood there, a gimpy grin on each face. Samuel held a covered pot. Adam had a covered plate in his hands.

"Come on in. What you got there?"

"Your supper. Ma figured you'd be a total slacker in the kitchen. She sent chicken and dumplings and baked bread so you don't kill Abigail in the meantime."

"Not nice," Luke warned. "Keep your voices down, she is still asleep."

"Sorry," Adam murmured. "You have to admit, seeing you in this domesticated role is quite hilarious."

The two brothers set the food on the table and began to laugh. Samuel even went as far as slapping his hand on his pant leg.

"It's not funny one bit. Get out, both of you!"

"That's no way to treat your brothers, who, by the way, brought you a delicious meal."

"Out!" Luke knew better than to keep them here longer than necessary. He loved his brothers but the gleam in both their eyes spelled trouble.

"We're going." Samuel was the first to head towards the door. He made a face at Adam, who instantly followed behind. Luke didn't trust them one bit. They were up to something.

When he looked out a few minutes later, there was no sign of them anywhere. He supposed they weren't going to pull any shenanigans tonight. Since the sun had already faded, he wasn't able to see far into the distance. Figuring they went to the barn to play some cards, Luke took the pot of dumplings from the table. It was still warm but he wanted to let Abigail sleep a little bit longer.

He stirred the fires in the stove, thinking about their evening together. The doc said complete bed rest for a few days until she was sure the headaches were gone. When a flame shot out from the belly of the stove, Luke jumped back, catching himself before tumbling towards the ground. His knee hit the floor but he didn't fall.

He heard some rumbling, along with smirking and looked up to see two faces peering in the kitchen window. Sonofagun! His brothers were peeking in the window! Luke shot out the front door like nobody's business, catching up to the two as they high-tailed it through the yard.

Luke leaped off the porch, catching Adam's right shoulder and bringing him down first. He was acting as childish as his other brothers but it could not be helped. For some reason, when the three of them were together, this was their way.

When Samuel looked back to see the two wrestling on the ground, he ran back and jumped in the fray as well. Like always, the three wrestled until one of them called out to stop. Since none of them did at first, the carousing went on for a lot longer than anyone realized.

A giggle came from the porch, stopping Luke in mid-air. He had just been about to straddle his brother and force him to give up by holding hands behind his back.

He turned to the soft sound of Abigail's voice. She held her fingers in front of her mouth, holding back a laugh. The other hand held her head as if she were trying to keep it from hurting.

The moment he saw her, Luke ran towards the porch. "Abigail! You should not be out of bed." Before anyone moved, Luke scooped her in his arms and carried her over the threshold, placing her on the settee, the closest piece of furniture inside the door.

"Oh, Luke, I'm tired of lying in bed. Let me sit here for awhile."

He sat beside her, taking her hands in his own. "Are you sure? The doc said bed rest for the next few days."

She leaned against him, dropping her head to rest on his shoulder. "Bed rest doesn't mean I can't get out of bed."

"I tend to disagree. I think that is exactly what it means."

'Hmm, well, then I will go back to bed after supper. I was lying there and something smelled so delicious."

"Ma sent over some chicken and dumplings. I'll carry you to the table."

Abigail smiled, resting a hand on his chest. "Luke, I believe I can walk. Nothing happened to my feet."

She went to stand up but he was there ahead of her. He scooped her in his arms again even though she insisted she was able to walk and sat her down in the chair at the head of the table. "Don't move, I'll get you a plate of food."

Luke hurried to the stove where the food was simmering. He was busy spooning out food when Abigail spoke up.

"Are you going to invite your brothers inside?" Her soft voice, even though it sounded weak, held a glimmer of humor.

Luke turned to find his two brothers peeking around the door frame. "I should've slammed that door shut with my boot," he grumbled. "You two, get on out of here. Go home."

"Let them stay. There's plenty for everyone."

At her soft-spoken words, Adam and Samuel came through the door as if they were invited by royalty. Luke tried to stare them down but they were too busy thanking Abigail for the invitation to eat.

Luke prepared a plate for Abigail and him, then sat down at the table. The two brothers looked on in surprise. "I am not your keeper, you want to eat, help yourself," Luke told them. He ignored the two as they scooted their chairs back and got their own plates.

"Abigail, are you sure you feel good enough to be up and about?" His question drew a slight smile from her.

"I'm fine, Luke. You worry too much."

"He sure does. Why, I've never seen this side of my brother before." Adam jumped in the conversation after folding his hands together in silent prayer.

"I'll say," Samuel agreed while he stuffed his mouth with a dumpling.

"You two had better not say another word or I'm throwing you out by your pant tails." Luke had enough of their nonsense.

"Your wife invited us to sit and eat, Luke. Don't upset her."

"It's true. Please don't get your wife upset." Samuel wasn't going to let Adam be the only one to mention the fact they had been invited to the supper table.

"Boys, please. Let's give my husband a break."

"Yes, ma'am," Adam told her, instantly keeping his nose down and eating his food.

Samuel followed suit, not saying another word.

After ten minutes of complete silence from his brothers, Luke raised a chin and grinned. His wife had shut the two of them up in three seconds flat. He squeezed her hand, then laid a gentle kiss on her cheek. Yes, sir, it was going to be mighty fine having Abigail around.

Chapter 10

Abigail sat outside on the rocker while waiting for Luke to come home. It had been a week and a half since the fiasco with the pup. She was feeling much stronger but he made her promise not to overdo things.

He had been the most attentive man, seeing to her needs and treating her as if she were a princess. It had taken her almost a week to feel back to normal and knowing he wasn't going to send her back to Miss Addie made everything more real.

This was her life now. They had their own home on the ranch, along with being able to live amongst family members who cared about the property and each other. Adam and Samuel were the sweetest brother-in-laws ever, even though Luke was constantly chasing them away. She had worked out a deal with them to bake a delicious pie and invite them to supper once a week if they stopped teasing Luke about how he fawned all over her.

So far the deal was being honored by the two. Although she had seen some carousing a few days ago near the apple orchard, Nora told her that had been going on from the time they were kids. From her vantage point on the front porch, she'd watch them come in from the range, some nights later than usual if they had a lot of work to do. Some evenings they came from different directions but always met near the apple orchard to talk. It was almost as if they weren't able to let a day go past without having a group meeting. It was almost as if they held a secret that only the three of them knew.

Abigail smiled. She had been an only child. Her parents had tried to force her into a marriage with someone so old it made her shiver. That's why she left to become a mail order bride. Now, watching the three brothers gathered at the orchard, she smiled to herself, then looked up.

Thank you, Lord. You did know what was best for me after all. Maybe eventually she'd send a letter to let her parents know she was well and much cared for even though she doubted they cared enough to write back. Unless she was able to give them something of monetary value, she didn't believe they cared about her well-being. All those years of feeling unloved made the last few weeks being loved worthwhile. If it hadn't been for coming here, she'd never have known Luke's love and adoration.

Supper was simmering on the cook stove, not quite ready to serve yet. Abigail grimaced, at least Luke had allowed her to cook. At first, all he wanted her to do was sit and behave herself. When she told Nora this bit of information, the older woman gave him a what for and ordered him back out on the range. "You're driving your wife and everyone else crazy! Doc James was here yesterday and said she is fine," his mother had told him. "If the good Lord was going to take her, he'd have done it that day. Now you go on back to work and don't come home until your brothers do!"

Abigail smiled, remembering how forlorn Luke seemed leaving her that day. She had to reassure him over and over again she was fine without him being there to watch over her. Although it was adorable to see him like this, she had to admit it was getting tiresome. He had gone from one extreme to the other and rather quickly. She wanted her adorable, confident, strutting Luke back.

She watched as he rode with his brothers towards the corral and barn, walking the horses before taking them inside. After awhile, he came out, waved to his brothers and picked some bluebonnets from the yard.

Abigail looked around her porch. There were little cups filled with bluebonnets all over the porch. Every single day he brought more home. She didn't have the heart to tell him they were being over run by flowers. It was a sweet gesture and she loved him more for being so thoughtful.

The closer he got, Abigail wanted to tell him she was ready to become truly married in all sense of the word. She wanted them to become man and wife in the marriage bed. He was so overprotective right now, she hoped this wasn't the way their whole marriage was going to be, otherwise she'd have to have words with him.

He stopped about four feet from the porch and tilted his head, smiling at her. "A penny for your thoughts?" he inquired.

She twisted her hands together, trying to figure out how to tell him her thoughts at hand. When he noticed, Luke was up on the porch by her side in two seconds flat. He sat down and took her in his arms. "What is it? Is something wrong?"

She leaned her head on his chest, a gesture that was becoming more of a habit lately. "Nothing is wrong, Luke. I don't know how to go about explaining this to you."

He kissed her on the head. "Let's eat supper and discuss things. I don't want you getting all excited."

She looked up at him then because that's exactly what she wanted to do. "I don't want to eat quite yet. I have it simmering on the stove."

Luke looked at her, taking her chin between his thumb and finger and moving her head so she looked directly in to his eyes. "Then, let's talk. Tell me, what's wrong?"

Abigail grinned. "I think there is something simmering besides the pot on the stove."

She saw his eyes flicker the moment it dawned on him. "That a fact?"

"It's a fact. And it is high time we stopped this nonsense about me being too fragile. I want you to make me your true wife right here, right now!"

Luke sat back and grinned. "Here? Out here on the porch?"

Abigail flung her head back and laughed out loud. "Oh, dear! Luke, you are kidding me, right? I, yikes! Luke! Put me down!"

Luke swept her in his arms and marched through the front door. This time he took his boot and kicked the door closed, then pushed a chair in front of the door. "No one is getting in here tonight," he told her.

"Oh, Luke, I love you!"

She waited for his words of love to come but he was too busy nuzzling her neck as he kicked shut the bedroom door as well.

When Luke told her to wear her Sunday best, she was so nervous, wondering what in the world he had planned for her today. She had noticed there was quite a bit of commotion going on at the main ranch house. "Is Nora having a party?" Abigail wondered why Nora hadn't said anything to her.

Luke stood by the front door, wearing a matching jacket and slacks, along with a long sleeve button down shirt. "It's a surprise and you are the recipient."

"Me? Oh, dear!" Her hand went to her dress to make sure everything was in place. She wore a pale blue and white gown, the color of the sky, with a skirt that trailed behind. Not a good choice for working on a ranch but she had brought it along none-the-less. Abigail secured the matching gloves and held out her hand. Her husband placed a soft kiss on her gloved hand. "You look beautiful, as always."

Abigail blushed. "You tell me this every single day. Thank you."

"I mean it every single day." He nuzzled her neck before securing the door as they went to ride up to the main house in the buggy.

As Luke turned the horse and buggy towards the back of the yard, Abigail was stunned and surprised at all the people there. How did she not see the wagons, buggies and horses lined up in the yard? Maybe because her husband had kept her very busy all morning long.

After careful scrutiny, she noticed most of the vehicles were hiding around the side of the barn where she was unable to see from her vantage point at their cabin. "Is this some sort of surprise?"

Her husband gloated. "It is. For you. For us. Our wedding reception."

Abigail let a tear fall. Luke took a thumb and wiped it from her cheek. "Don't cry, darling. It's time to celebrate." He turned her towards him, gently brushing her lips with his own. "I love you, Abigail. This day is for you. I wanted to show you how much you are loved."

She flung her arms around his neck, not caring if she wrinkled her beautiful dress. His words meant the world to her. She felt as if she were home, as if this place had called out to her.

Two handsome men in matching suits walked towards them. Abigail gave them both a hug. "Thank you, Adam, Samuel, for helping with this surprise."

Samuel blushed while Adam wasn't paying attention. He was busy searching the crowd. Abigail followed his gaze when it stopped at Melody and her red-headed little boy. She shifted, uncomfortable when she realized the look on her brother-in-laws face was one of longing for a woman he couldn't have. It made her sad to know this. They had been best friends growing up, Abigail was told, but the look on his face said so much more.

Nora rushed towards them. "Welcome, you two! I see Luke's told you about your special day. I love you both so much!" Nora took them both in a big hug, kissing Abigail on the cheek. "How lovely! You've chosen the most beautiful gown to wear to today's celebration. We've got so much in store for the two of you. Come along now, let me show you."

Abigail and Luke spent the next few hours mingling with neighbors and other folk who stopped by to join in the festivities. There wasn't much else in the way of celebrations since most people lived far from Wichita Falls but on a Saturday afternoon, no one minded getting dressed for a celebration like this. Tons of food filled up the long tables Nora had laid out. A large white cake took up over half the area on one table.

Rusty and three older gentleman began to play their instruments as the day began to wear on. A few of the children danced around the yard. When a soft melody began to play, Luke took her hand and guided her to the center, in front of the musicians. His hands went to her waist and he held her closer than it was proper to do so.

She whispered in his ear. "You're going to have the whole countryside talking about this dance," she teased him. The truth was, Abigail didn't care what anyone thought or said. All she knew was the feeling of being in her husband's arms. The way he held her right now topped anything she'd ever felt in her life.

"I want the whole world to know how much you mean to me."

She hugged him tighter. "I feel the same."

Luke swore. "What are they doing here?" he burst out, slowing his feet until the two stood still.

Abigail turned her head to see Widow Young and her two sons standing by one of the food tables, speaking with Nora. Their heads were close together as if they were having much more than a casual conversation.

Luke glanced around the area, nodding to Adam. When Adam turned to see what was wrong, his eyes widened. He grabbed Samuel, who was a few feet away and headed towards the table area. Luke shook his head. "I'm sorry, Abigail. I'll be right back. Can you go get something to quench your thirst?"

"Certainly. What's wrong? Can I help?" Abigail became worried. The whole situation was beginning to have her concerned. Why were all three of the brothers making their way towards Nora? She stood dead still, watching the three until little Tommy stood in front of her holding Trouble in his arms.

"Abigail?" A little voice cut into her thoughts. She knelt down closer.

"What do you have here, Tommy?"

"Trouble wanted to come with me. My momma said I had to ask you first."

She smiled, forgetting about the trio. "Of course it is fine. But, Tommy, you have to watch him very carefully. Are you able to do that?"

He nodded his head, the red curls bouncing faster than his head was going. "I promise. Maybe it will make momma happy again."

Abigail tilted her head. "Oh? Why do you say that, Tommy?"

He shrugged. "I'm not supposed to tell."

"Why not, Tommy?" The little boy had her complete attention. She adored Melody and if there was something going on, something happening that Abigail could help her with, she wanted to know.

"Can I get Trouble some of the food over there?" He pointed to the table loaded with a variety of dishes as the little pup wiggled in his arms.

"Hold on to him with two hands, Tommy. Yes, you can feed him but first tell me why your momma isn't happy."

He looked towards his mom then took a step closer and whispered in her ear. "Cause she is getting a der-voice."

Abigail tried to keep a straight face while Tommy struggled to get the words out. Then it dawned on her. Her eyes widened in surprise and shock. "Do you mean a divorce?"

He nodded again. "Yes, yes, ma'am. My daddy is a cheating no good snake."

"Oh, Tommy. I don't think you should mention this to anyone else, OK? Go on now, take Trouble to get something to eat."

Abigail gave Melody a worried look. She was hesitant to speak with her about the impending divorce. It was obvious Melody didn't want anyone to know.

Then Melody happened to look up. She shifted in her seat, a worried look on her face. Abigail couldn't help herself. She made her way to her friend and sat beside her. "Melody, you don't look well. Is everything alright?"

Melody attempted a brave smile but Abigail knew better. "I'm fine, and you?"

She was trying hard to keep the subject off herself but she wanted Melody to know she had someone who supported her no matter what. "I'm also fine, better than fine. Melody, I'll be honest. Tommy spilled the beans about what is happening."

Melody cringed. Her face paled and her eyes darted back and forth. Abigail spoke low to make sure no one nearby was able to hear.

"Please! Don't tell a soul. Promise me! Promise!"

Abigail was worried Melody would faint dead away. Her skin paled even more at the thought of someone knowing about her situation. It wasn't something to announce as people tended to frown upon a divorced woman these days. Even in Philadelphia it wasn't too common for a marriage to end in divorce. The courts always decided and many were not granted. "I promise. I want you to promise me something in exchange for my silence."

"Oh, Abigail. I can't promise anything right now. I'm ruined. There will be a trial next week and I'm so afraid he will try to keep Tommy for spite. I'll give up everything I own, sell my soul to the devil if he agrees to let me keep my child."

Abigail's heart cringed at the thought of Melody and Tommy split apart. She saw in just this short time how close they were. She took Melody's hand in hers. "Promise me when this is all over, when you get a divorce and custody of your son, you will come here the moment it is done. Promise me this and I will keep your secret."

Melody sighed. She nodded. "I promise."

Abigail stood when she noticed her husband searching for her. She gave Melody a hug. "I'll see you soon. Remember, I'll keep my word and so will you."

Melody stood and hugged her back. "Thank you. I haven't told a soul. When Miss Nora invited us to your celebration she was shocked my husband didn't come in on the train, too. I said he was out of town working. I hated to lie but I can't tell anyone yet. It's so horrific even if it is a relief that you know and not judge me. When this is all over,

I know everyone in Dallas will treat me differently. I will no longer be welcomed there and Tommy will be shunned and ridiculed."

"That's why you need to come back here to the ranch. I'll be waiting for you."

Abigail turned to her husband when he came up alongside her. He looked at her, a curious and stern look on his face. Oh, dear, Abigail thought, what had happened with the Youngs? She glanced back to the tables where they had been standing but the lot of them were nowhere to be found. A buggy was leaving down the road and she was almost certain the Youngs were on it.

She took her husband's hand. "Why are you frowning?"

He shook his head. "I didn't see you at first."

Abigail knew he was avoiding the subject but she wasn't willing to compromise the rest of their celebration by worrying about this and that. Whatever happened with the Youngs was plainly none of her business or her husband would tell her.

Just as she was going to keep the secret of Melody's divorce, she felt in her soul that something strange was going on between the Whites and the Youngs. Perhaps he had made a promise to himself, or his brothers or even his mother. Was Nora in this secret as well?

She didn't know. Scanning the crowd, Abigail watched her mother-in-law as she mingled. If she hadn't been watching her, she'd have missed the way Nora turned to check on each one of her boys with a concerned look on her face. Abigail tried to push the thought back. It wasn't her business.

"Penny for your thoughts?" her husband asked. He placed his strong arms around her, moving them both to the sound of the ballad that began to play. Other couples joined them on the lawn, even some kids trying to dance like the adults.

Abigail looked around. She gazed at the vast land in front and behind her, watched as the sun began to set on the horizon, it's bright yellow glow turning orange as it faded away. She heard the musicians playing, the neighbors chatting and laughing while wondering how she had gotten so lucky. "I feel like the luckiest woman in the world," she told him, placing a kiss before he could say a word.

He deepened the kiss, showing her how much he loved her. "You are the most loved woman in the world, there's no luck to that, it's a blessing from above," he said between kisses. "I love you, Abigail.

"I love you, too, Luke. I can't wait to have children with you." Luke began to lower his mouth to hers for a second time when a head popped over his shoulder.

"I love you, too, brother." Samuel's voice cackled. He began chuckling, wrapping his arm around his brother's shoulders.

"Oh, I love you too, honey," Adam quipped, laughing out loud at the look on Luke's face.

Luke shook his head. He didn't want to ruin his wedding celebration but there were just some things a man could not tolerate. Like his brothers always trying to ridicule. Well, they were teasing and it was all in fun. Neither one of them were able to help themselves at times like this.

"Today is the happiest day of my life and of course you two are going to try to -" He moved Abigail out of the way. " Adam! Samuel!"

Nora hurried towards them. "Abigail! Get out of the way! Boys!"

Abigail stepped back, clutching her stomach, laughing hard. She knew what was about to happen. It couldn't be helped. The men would always be boys. Brothers to the end.

<> <> <> <>

Thank you for reading the first book in the Sons of Nora White series, A Bride For Luke.

The next book, *A Bride For Adam* is about the long-term friendship between Adam and Melody. When her divorce becomes final, the city of Dallas practically shuns her and her son. She had promised Abigail she'd come back to the White Ranch. She needed her family, her friends and most of all her best-friend. Except he was getting ready to find himself his own mail-order bride and she didn't dare stand in his way of true happiness.

When Adam realizes Melody is divorced, his true feelings come to light. Except a mail order bride is on her way to the ranch to marry him. He sends Samuel to divert the bride, hoping he can figure out what to do before he marries the wrong woman.

Then there is the family secret never to be shared with anyone outside of the three brothers. Can Adam keep it a secret or will he spill the beans to his best friend?

A BRIDE FOR ADAM IS AVAILABLE NOW![1]

(https://www.amazon.com/gp/product/B079WQG73H/

ref=as_li_ss_tl?ie=UTF8&linkCode=ll1&tag=keysvaca-20&linkId=268

OR

If you'd like to read all 4 stories in one shot, get Cyndi's box set that includes the first 4 stories of the Sons of Nora White

Sons of Nora White box Set Volume 1-4[2] (https://amzn.to/ 39xadwm)

---

1. https://www.amazon.com/gp/product/B079WQG73H/

   ref=as_li_ss_tl?ie=UTF8&linkCode=ll1&tag=keysvaca-20&linkId=268e65bfad

   2b2efa06f93994b01e4d29&language=en_US

2. https://amzn.to/39xadwm

<> <> <> <>

I love being active with my readers. Come on over to my facebook group, Cyndi[3]Raye[4] Readers. [5](https://www.facebook.com/groups/1856224058000936/)

To find out more about Cyndi's books, keep reading....

---

3. https://www.facebook.com/groups/1856224058000936/

4. https://www.facebook.com/groups/1856224058000936/

5. https://www.facebook.com/groups/1856224058000936/

Reading Order of Cyndi's books
Brides of Wichita Falls
Ruby
Grace
Lily
Charity
Hannah
Rebecca
Sophie
Ellie
Jenna
Leila
Vol 1-8 Boxed Set
Christmas in Wichita Falls
Brides of Mill Ridge
An Outlaw's Honor
A Reverend's Rose
The Ranger's Redemption
A Doctor's Devotion
A Teacher's Treasure
A Sister's Sanctuary

Sons of Nora White Series
Sons Boxed set
A Bride for Luke
A Bride for Adam
A Bride for Samuel
A Groom for Nora
A Bride for Russell
A Bride for Wesley
A Groom for Widow Young
You can find all these books and more at
Cyndi's Amazon Page[1] (**https://www.amazon.com/**

Cyndi-Raye/e/B00ENA1WEG)

---

1. https://www.amazon.com/Cyndi-Raye/e/B00ENA1WEG

Don't miss out!

Visit the website below and you can sign up to receive emails whenever Cyndi Raye publishes a new book. There's no charge and no obligation.

https://books2read.com/r/B-A-PXQ-VXVFC

BOOKS 2 READ

Connecting independent readers to independent writers.